Sherryl
Woods

A Chesapeake
Shores Christmas

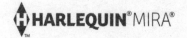
HARLEQUIN®MIRA®

First published in Great Britain 2012
Harlequin MIRA, an imprint of Harlequin (UK) Limited,
Eton House, 18-24 Paradise Road,
Richmond, Surrey, TW9 1SR

© Sherryl Woods 2010

ISBN 978 1 848 45158 2

58-1112

Harlequin's policy is to use papers that are natural, renewable and recyclable products and made from wood grown in sustainable forests. The logging and manufacturing processes conform to the legal environmental regulations of the country of origin.

Printed and bound by
CPI Group (UK) Ltd, Croydon, CR0 4YY

Dear Friends,

Here is your chance to see Mick and Megan O'Brien's long-awaited reconciliation. Watching these two stubborn people—arguably the most stubborn in a family of mule-headed folks—reunite after so many years apart sets up the perfect situation in need of a holiday miracle or two.

It's especially tricky with Connor, their younger son, determined to stand in their way. Connor, as you may know, has a few issues of his own to worry about, though, which may give Mick just the manoeuvring room he needs to get Megan to the altar.

I hope the reconciliation is worth the wait. I also hope you'll be looking for the next instalment in the Chesapeake Shores series, *Driftwood Cottage*, in stores in June 2013.

In the meantime, I wish you the happiest of holidays and all the blessings of the season!

Sherryl Woods

1

It was only the second time in the more than twelve years since her divorce that Megan O'Brien had been home in Chesapeake Shores during the holiday season.

Newly divorced and separated from her children, Megan had found the memories had been too bittersweet to leave New York and come back for Christmas. She'd tried to make up for her absence by sending a mountain of presents, each one carefully chosen to suit the interests of each child. She'd called on Christmas Day, but the conversations with the older children had been grudging and too brief. Her youngest, Jess, had refused to take her call at all.

The following year Megan had ventured back to town, hoping to spend time with the children on Christmas morning. Her ex-husband, Mick O'Brien, had agreed to the visit. She'd anticipated seeing their eyes light up over the presents she'd chosen. She'd even arranged for a special breakfast at Brady's, a family favorite, but the atmosphere had been so strained, the reaction to her gifts so dismissive, that she'd driven everyone back home an hour later. She'd managed to hide her tears and disappointment until she was once again alone in her hotel room.

After that, she'd made countless attempts to convince the children to come to New York for the holidays, but they'd stubbornly refused, and Mick had backed them up. She could have fought harder, but she'd realized that to do so would only ruin Christmas for all of them. Teenagers who were where they didn't want to be could make everyone's life miserable.

Now she parked her car at the end of Main and walked slowly along the block, taking it all in. Even though it was only days after Halloween, the town was all decked out. Every storefront along Main

Street had been transformed with twinkling white lights and filled with enticing displays. The yellow chrysanthemums outside the doorways during the fall had given way to an abundance of bright red poinsettias.

Workers were stringing lights along the downtown streets and readying a towering fir on the town green for a tree-lighting ceremony that would be held in a few weeks. The only thing missing was snow, and since Chesapeake Shores hadn't had a white Christmas in years, no one was counting on that to set the scene. The town created its own festive atmosphere to charm residents and lure tourists to the seaside community.

As she strolled, Megan recalled the sweet simplicity of going Christmas shopping with the kids when they were small, pausing as they stared in wonder at the window displays. There were a few new shops now, but many remained exactly the same, the windows gaily decorated in a suitable theme. Now it was her grandchildren who would be enchanted by the displays.

Ethel's Emporium, for instance, still had the same animated figures of Santa and Mrs. Claus in the window along with giant jars filled with the colorful penny candy that was so popular with the children in town. Once again, Seaside Gifts had draped fishing nets in the window, woven lights through them and added an exceptional assortment of glittering nautical ornaments, some delicate, some delightfully gaudy and outrageous.

At her daughter Bree's shop, Flowers on Main, lights sparkled amid a sea of red and white poinsettias. Next door, in her daughter-in-law Shanna's bookstore, the window featured seasonal children's books, along with a selection of holiday cookie recipe books and a plate filled with samples to entice a jolly life-size stuffed Santa. Inside, she knew, there would be more of the delectable cookies for the customers. The chef at her daughter Jess's inn was sending them over daily during the season, some packaged for resale as enticing gifts.

In fact, all along Main Street, Megan saw evidence of her family settling down in this town that had been the creation of her ex-husband, architect Mick O'Brien. Though all of their children except Jess had fled for careers and college, one by one they had drifted back home and made lives for themselves in Chesapeake Shores. They'd made peace with their father and, to some extent, with her. Only Connor, now an attorney in Baltimore, had kept his distance.

It should have been gratifying to see an O'Brien touch everywhere she looked, but instead it left Megan feeling oddly out of sorts. Just like Connor, she, too, had yet to find her way home. And though her relationship with Mick had been improving— she had, in fact, agreed to consider marrying him again—something continued to hold her back from making that final commitment.

Megan shivered as the wind off the Chesapeake Bay cut through her. Though it was nothing like the wind that whipped between New York's skyscrapers this time of year, the bitter chill and gathering storm clouds seemed to accentuate her odd mood.

When she shivered again, strong arms slid around her waist from behind and she was drawn into all the protective warmth that was Mick O'Brien. He smelled of the crisp outdoors and the lingering aroma of a spicy aftershave, one as familiar to her as the scent of sea air.

"Why the sad expression, Meggie?" he asked. "Isn't this the most wonderful time of the year? You used to love Christmas."

"I still do," she said, leaning against him. Despite

all those sorrowful holidays she'd spent alone, it was impossible for her to resist the hopeful magic of the season. "New York is always so special during the holidays. I'd forgotten that Chesapeake Shores has its own charm at Christmas."

She gestured toward the shop windows. "Bree and Shanna have a real knack for creating inviting displays, don't they?"

"Best on the block," he said proudly. There was nothing an O'Brien did that wasn't the best, according to Mick—unless, of course, it was an accomplishment by one of his estranged brothers, Jeff or Thomas. "Why don't we go to Sally's and have some hot chocolate and one of her raspberry croissants?"

"I was planning to start on my Christmas shopping this morning," she protested. "It's practically my duty to support the local economy, don't you think?"

"Why not warm up with the hot chocolate first?" he coaxed. "And then I'll go with you."

Megan regarded him with surprise. "You hate to shop."

"That was the old me," he said with the irrepressible grin she'd never been able to resist. "I'm reformed, remember? I want to do anything that allows me some extra time with you. Besides, I'm hoping you'll give me some ideas about what you really want for Christmas."

Given all the years when Mick had turned his holiday shopping over to her and later to his secretary, this commitment to finding the perfect gift was yet more evidence that he was truly trying to change his neglectful ways.

"I appreciate the thought," she began, only to draw a scowl.

"Don't be telling me you don't need anything," he said as he guided her into Sally's. "Christmas gifts aren't about what you need. They're about things that will make those beautiful eyes of yours light up."

Megan smiled. "You still have the gift of blarney, Mick O'Brien." And over the past couple of years since they'd been reunited, his charm had become harder and harder to resist. In fact, she couldn't say for sure why she'd been so reluctant to set a wedding date when he'd shown her time and again how much he'd tried to change in all the ways that had once mattered so much to her.

When they were seated and held steaming cups of hot chocolate, topped with extra marshmallows, she studied the man across from her. Still handsome, with thick black hair, twinkling blue eyes and a body kept fit from working construction in many of his own developments as well as his recent Habitat for Humanity projects, Mick O'Brien would turn any woman's head.

Now when he was with her—unlike when they were married—he was attentive and thoughtful. He courted her as only a man who knew her deepest desires possibly could. There was an intimacy and understanding between them that could only come from so many years of marriage.

And yet, she still held back. She'd found so many excuses, in fact, that Mick had stopped pressing her to set a date. She had a feeling that a perverse desire to be pursued was behind her disgruntled mood this morning.

"You've that sad expression on your face again, Meggie. Is something wrong?" he asked, once more proving he was attuned to her every mood.

She drew in a deep breath and, surprising herself, blurted, "I'm wondering why you've stopped pestering me to marry you."

At the question, Mick's expression immediately brightened. "Are you saying you've finally run out of excuses?"

"Possibly," she said, then gave him a challenging look. "Try me."

A sheepish smile spread across his face. "Well, for starters, you should know that I have New Year's Eve on hold at Jess's inn," he admitted. "Just in case."

Startled, Megan stared at him. "For our wedding?"

"Or at least a family party, if I couldn't coax you into finally saying yes to a wedding date," he said hurriedly. "What do you think, Meggie? Would you like to start the new year as Mrs. Mick O'Brien? I know for me there'd be no better time to begin the next stage of our life together."

He reached across the table and clasped her hand. "Will you marry me so we can greet the new year together? Say yes and we'll go straight to the jewelry store where I have the perfect ring on hold. Sapphires and diamonds that sparkle like your eyes. I knew the minute I saw it that it belonged on your hand."

It had taken Megan a long time to get over all the times Mick had gone running off for work, abandoning her to care for their five children alone. It had taken years for her to understand that the neglect had been born not just of ego but of a powerful drive to provide for his family. She'd forgiven him long ago. Now it was simply a question of ignoring all the lingering doubts that crept in late at night, when she was alone in her bed in New York, and taking a leap of faith into the future he was offering, to believe it wouldn't turn out the same way as the past.

She took a deep breath and made the leap. "I think New Year's Eve would be a wonderful time to get married," she said, her eyes blurred by tears.

Mick frowned. "If it's so wonderful, why are you crying?"

"Because I'm happy," she said, deliberately pushing her lingering doubts aside. She was stronger now. She'd found a career of her own in New York, one she could bring with her to Chesapeake Shores. She could be an equal partner with Mick this time. Not everything would have to be on his terms. They'd finally have the life she'd envisioned the first time they'd married.

Obviously satisfied by her answer, Mick immediately grabbed his coat and stood, then reached for her hand. "Let's go."

She regarded him with bafflement. "Where? We just got here. I've barely taken a sip of this hot chocolate you were so intent on having."

"We can get more to go. Right now, we have a ring to buy, people to tell, plans to make and not a lot of time." Already waving for the check, he ticked off a list. "We'll stop in to see Bree and order the flowers, then see if Kevin's at the bookstore with Shanna and we can tell them the news."

There he was, barreling ahead with his plans, not two seconds after she'd envisioned a real partnership. Megan regarded him with dismay. "Slow down, Mick. Shouldn't we tell everyone at once? Maybe invite them all over for dinner and make a big announcement? And there's Nell. We don't want your mother hearing this from anyone else in the family. She's sensitive enough about the idea of me coming back and taking over after all her years of running your home. We want to settle how this will work, so she won't feel as if I'm displacing her. After all she's done for this family, we owe her that much consideration."

After a moment's hesitation, Mick sighed and sat back down. "You were always the sensible one," he said.

"And you were always the passionate one with big ideas he expected everyone to go along with," she said. "We need to keep in mind that even though things are better with our children, they may not be as overjoyed about this as we are."

"Abby's been plotting exactly this for a very long time," he reminded her.

Megan couldn't deny that their eldest child had played a role in bringing them back together. "She may be the only one with a longing to see us reunited," she observed realistically.

"They're all adults. They'll just have to deal with it," he said stubbornly.

"Now there's the sensitive side of you I've missed," she said wryly.

"Okay, okay, I see your point. We'll handle this your way," Mick grumbled. "But nobody's standing in our way. I won't allow it."

Megan grinned. "Famous last words."

Mick managed to feign enthusiasm for Christmas shopping for an hour, but Megan could see it was killing him. He simply didn't have the patience for it.

"Go home," she said eventually. "You know you hate this."

"I just don't understand why it takes so long to decide between one scarf and another," he grumbled. "You spent twenty minutes debating between the blue scarf and the red one, then wound up buying them both."

Megan laughed. "I was thinking how lovely the blue would be with your mother's eyes, but how much she'd enjoy wearing the red one during the holidays."

"Then why didn't you take them both in the first place?"

"I was trying to be frugal," she explained, then grinned. "Then I remembered you're rich. There's no reason not to give Nell two cashmere scarves she'll love. You'll give her one, I the other."

"Is it going to be like this with every person on your list?" he asked.

"More than likely, which is why you should go. You don't have the stamina required for truly dedicated Christmas shopping."

"But I want to spend the day with you," he protested. "You're not here nearly long enough. We need to talk about changing that as soon as possible. With all the decisions that need to be made about the wedding, you should be living here full-time."

She swallowed hard at the reminder of just how much her life was about to change. "I promise we'll talk about all that later," she said. "Give me one more hour to shop on my own, then I'll meet you."

His expression brightened. "At the jewelry store?"

"If you like, although if you're buying the engagement ring, shouldn't you pick it out on your own, then present it to me with some big flourish?"

"That's one way to go," he agreed. "But the last time I bought you a ring, you said it was too ostentatious and never wore it. Once this one's on your finger, it's going to stay there, so you might as well have a say in choosing it. It's one of those partnership decisions you're always going on about."

Megan chuckled. "Okay, fine. I'll be at the jewelry store in an hour. What will you be doing?"

"I think I'll stop by Ethel's and get some candy for our grandkids. I'm all out of the kind they like to find tucked in my pockets."

"I thought both Abby and Kevin told you to stop feeding their children candy every time you see them."

"Grandfather's prerogative," he said airily. "And don't be bugging me about that. I know you keep a stash of candy on hand for them, too. And Ma has her cookie jar filled with their favorites."

"Guilty," she admitted, then pressed a kiss to his cheek. "I do love you, Mick O'Brien."

She hurried off to the boutique on the next block, her step surprisingly light. The sky had turned clear blue, as if to match her improved mood. She just prayed that the hope and anticipation she was feeling right now could weather whatever reactions the rest of the family had to their news.

When the entire O'Brien family assembled for dinner these days, it took several extra leaves in the table and the patience of a saint to be heard over the commotion of the children. Normally Mick loved these family gatherings, especially now that Megan was so often a part of them again.

For too many years after his wife had left him, he hadn't been able to sit down in the dining room without feeling her absence as an ache in his heart. That's why he'd stayed away so much, using the excuse of work to avoid the emptiness he felt in his home.

He glanced down the length of the table, feeling a sense of satisfaction at seeing Abby and her twins, Carrie and Caitlyn, with Trace beside them, then Jake and Bree, who was expecting their first child. On the other side of the table were Kevin and his son, Davy, along with his new wife, Shanna, and their recently adopted boy, Henry. Connor was next to Kevin, giving grief to the youngest of them all, Jess, who'd finally found her niche in life running The Inn at Eagle Point. Nell, who'd cared for the children in Megan's absence, sat next to Jess, periodically scolding Connor just as she had so many times when they were children.

And then at the end, where she'd always belonged, was Megan. She, too, was studying their family with an expression of misty-eyed nostalgia. She lifted her gaze to meet his and smiled. Mick winked at her, then stood and tapped a spoon on his glass of wine until he drew everyone's attention.

"Okay, everybody, settle down," he said. "I have something to say."

"Uh-oh, somebody's in trouble," Connor taunted, his gaze immediately going to Jess.

"Not me," she insisted. "I've been an angel lately, right, Dad?"

"A perfect angel," Mick concurred. "And nobody's in trouble. Your mother and I have some news."

"You're getting married!" Abby exclaimed, shoving back her chair and hurrying to throw her arms around him.

As the oldest, Abby had done her best to fill a mother's shoes when Megan had left them. She'd also fought hard to bring about this reconciliation, though it had clearly taken far longer than she'd anticipated.

Mick staggered back with the exuberance of her hug, then chuckled. "Way to steal my thunder, girl."

Bree stared at him, wide-eyed, a mix of hope and dismay on her face. "It's true? You and Mom are getting married again?"

"On New Year's Eve," he confirmed as Megan lifted her left hand to display the ring he'd placed on it yesterday.

"That's why you wanted me to reserve the inn for a private party," Jess concluded. Like Bree, she seemed disconcerted by the news, but not entirely unhappy about it.

Abby released him and went to her mother. "Mom, I'm so happy for you. I know how long you've wanted this."

Bree dutifully made her way to Megan and hugged her, followed with slightly less exuberance by Jess. Kevin stood and shook Mick's hand.

"Congratulations, Dad!" he said with lukewarm enthusiasm. With obvious reluctance, he turned toward Megan. "You, too, Mother."

In the general commotion, it took a minute for Mick to note that Connor had remained totally silent. Mick caught his younger son's eye and saw a surprising amount of barely banked anger in his gaze.

"Connor? You've been awfully quiet," Mick said, giving him a warning look. "Isn't there something you want to say?"

Connor stood and cast a sour look at everyone else in the room before turning the brunt of his anger on Mick. "Are you all out of your flipping minds?" he demanded heatedly. "Have you forgotten that Mom ditched us all, Dad included? And now you're going to welcome her back so she can break all of our hearts again? Well, not me."

"Connor O'Brien!" Mick said, his voice booming in warning. "Keep a civil tongue in your head."

"Save the lecture, Dad," Connor retorted. "I'm out of here."

As he tore out of the room, Mick turned to Kevin. "Go after him," he ordered.

"No," Megan said, standing. She looked shaken, but determined. "I'll go."

"Mom, maybe that's not such a good idea," Abby protested.

"I'm the one he's unhappy with," Megan said. "It's up to me to fix it."

"She's right," Nell said, speaking for the first time. "Let her go."

Mick wanted to stop Megan, to do whatever was

necessary to protect her from more hurtful accusations, but he knew better than to try. "If that boy says one disrespectful word to you, if he—"

She gave him a chiding look. "I'll handle it. The rest of you enjoy this wonderful meal Nell fixed for us." She gave Nell's shoulder a squeeze before leaving the room.

Filled with regret, Mick watched her go. Abby returned to her seat beside him and patted his hand.

"It's going to be okay, Dad," she said, setting aside whatever reservations she'd had. "Mom will get through to Connor. She has with the rest of us."

Mick wanted to believe Abby was right, but he knew what the others might not understand. Connor's whole reason for becoming an attorney, the drive behind his success, was a grim determination to help other men get even for their wives' betrayals. He already had a reputation in his young career as the kind of attorney any man would want in his corner during a particularly acrimonious divorce. Mick couldn't help but be proud of his success, but he worried about the embittered motivation behind it.

On the surface, Connor had seemed like a typically carefree teen, taking Megan's departure in stride, but it had affected him deeply. It had left him jaded about marriage in general, and especially about Mick's marriage to Megan. During the divorce, when Mick had acquiesced to most of Megan's requests, when he'd supported her lifestyle in New York until she'd been able to pay her own way, Connor had viewed it as a sign of weakness. When Mick had told him he intended to do right by the mother of his children, Connor had told him he was a fool, then stormed from the house. Even as a young teen, he'd had a temper and a tendency to speak his mind. To this day he and Mick had an uneasy relationship because of his ill-considered remarks back then. Usually, though, he disguised his hostility behind a jovial facade that the others rarely saw through.

So, while it wasn't surprising that Connor wasn't happy about Mick's announcement, it was a shock to see the facade slip. Mick had hoped for a different reaction, but with Connor resentments ran deep. Since Mick had been carrying his own deep-seated grudges against his brothers for years, he understood how difficult it was to let go of the past. He'd just hoped for better from his son, for Megan's sake, if not his own.

One way or another, though, he wouldn't let Connor ruin what should be the happiest time of his life—the chance to finally get it right with Megan and bring his family back together. If Megan couldn't get Connor to listen to reason, Mick would. One way or another, the O'Briens were going to celebrate the new year with a wedding. He'd see to it.

2

Megan caught up with Connor as he was trying to start his car. She slid into the passenger side of the expensive two-seater sports car and closed the door, then gave him a defiant look.

"Wherever you're headed, you're stuck with me," she told him.

He scowled at her, but when she didn't budge, he shrugged. "Suit yourself."

He threw the car into gear and shot out of the driveway and along the coastal road at a pace Megan knew was designed to terrify her. She clung to the door and kept silent until they reached town, where he was forced to slow down. He pulled to a stop in a parking space on Shore Road facing the bay, his jaw set, his scowl firmly in place.

"Feel better?" she inquired. "You do know that getting us killed probably won't solve anything."

"At least you wouldn't get to marry Dad and ruin his life again," he said, his tone petulant.

"Does your father seem as if his life's ruined?"

"Maybe not, but only because he's living in a dreamworld right now. Just wait till you take off again."

"Maybe what we really need to talk about is how I ruined *your* life," she suggested. "That's what this is actually about."

"You're irrelevant to my life. You have been for years."

Megan blinked back tears at the deliberately cruel words. "If I truly meant nothing to you, you wouldn't sound so bitter," she said quietly. She tilted her head and studied him. "You've fooled us all, you know. You have this easy, lighthearted way about you, but I think hurts run even more deeply. You're like your father that way."

"Don't try analyzing me, Mother. You don't know anything about me."

"Is that so?" she countered. "Let's see. I know you graduated at the top of your class from college, that you could have played pro baseball, but chose to go to law school. I know that you won a highly coveted job as a law clerk with a top Baltimore firm. I know when one of the senior partners was getting a divorce, he chose you to represent him and bragged that he'd never seen anyone fight harder for a client." She gave Connor an assessing look. "I assume that was because you saw me in his wife and your father in him. Obviously my divorce from your father was good for something."

Connor looked faintly surprised by her recitation. "What, did you hire a private detective to dig up all that information when you started seeing Dad again? You must have figured you'd need a way to worm your way back into all our lives."

Megan sighed. "I didn't need to hire anybody, Connor. I've kept tabs on each of you. Abby and I grew close again after she moved to New York. I went to Chicago to see Bree's plays. I even came to a few of your college ball games."

He snorted with disbelief.

"Remember the game against Carolina?" she said. "You hit an inside-the-park home run, and when you slid into home base, you broke your wrist." She shuddered at the memory of his face contorted with pain. "It took everything in me not to run to you on the field."

"You could have read about that in the paper," he said.

"I could have," she agreed. "Or someone in the family could have mentioned it to me. But if I'd found out either of those ways, would I have known that a pretty blonde cheerleader left with you in the ambulance?"

He sighed and closed his eyes. "Okay, fine. You were there. Big deal."

"It was for me," she said quietly. "Knowing that I had no right to come to you even when you were hurt tore me apart, Connor."

"So it was all about you, as usual."

"No, it was about *you,* and knowing that you wouldn't have appreciated me showing up out of the blue at the hospital. It's always been about you and your sisters and Kevin. Everything I did, I did because I thought it was for the best for you. Even leaving your father."

"Oh, no," he said. "You can't spin that now. Leaving was all about you, Mother. You can't deny that. You didn't give a second thought to what it would be like for us after you ran off to make an exciting new life for yourself."

"Okay, I'll admit that I needed to leave and build a new life for myself, but I thought that would be better for all of you, too. You wouldn't have a mother who resented your father the way I did. You'd have one who was strong and sure of herself again."

"That sounds to me as if it was all about you."

"Well, it wasn't," she said defensively. "Surely you know by now that I planned for all of you to come to New York with me. I had rooms ready, schools picked out. I even had your father's blessing."

"Funny, but I don't recall spending even a day in New York."

"Because you and Kevin took your father's side and refused to consider moving. You didn't want to leave your friends. You wouldn't even spend time with me when I visited you here. Abby said she wasn't going anywhere without Jess and Bree, and they threw fits at the thought of leaving Chesapeake Shores. Your father and I finally agreed to give it more time, to start with visits."

"How'd that work out? I've been to New York a dozen times, and never once did I see you," Connor retorted.

"Because you turned down every invitation," she reminded him quietly. "And I don't recall you phoning on any of those visits you made, either. Relationships work both ways, Connor, even between parents and their nearly grown children. Every time I knew you were coming—and I did know about most of those trips—I sat by the phone, hoping against hope that this would be the time you'd reach out to me."

"So now you're the neglected saint of a mother and I'm the terrible son?"

She gave him a pitying look. "Oh, Connor, no. I'm just trying to make you see that there are two sides to every story. You have your perspective, and I have mine. The truth is probably somewhere in the middle. Don't you think it would be worth it to try to find it, to make peace after all this time? I'm still your mother, and I've always loved you."

"How convenient that you've discovered this maternal love after all these years!"

"Do I need to remind you of the time I devoted to you, to all of you, before I left?"

"Give me a break, Mother. This is all about stopping us from interfering with your plan to marry Dad again, your scheme to take advantage of him. I won't allow it, you know. There will be a prenup this time. I'll see to it."

"Fine," she said readily. "Bring it on. I'll sign it happily, though I think your father might have other ideas. My relationship with your father has never been about money. We were church-mouse poor when we started out."

"But not by the time you left," he reminded her. "You were happy enough to take a bundle of his money so you could live in New York."

"I took only what was necessary to find a place that would be a good environment for you children," she corrected. "When you didn't come, I moved into a smaller place and never took another dime from him." She met his gaze. "Did you know that? I've paid my own way for years now, Connor. That's not going to stop if your father and I marry."

He seemed startled by the news. "You're planning to work?" he scoffed. "Doing what?"

"My boss and I have been discussing the possibility of me opening a branch of his art gallery here. Now that your father and I have set a wedding date,

I'll speak to Phillip about proceeding with that." She gave him a steady look. "Any other concerns?"

"A boatload of them, but I'm sure you'll have an answer for everything," he said sourly.

"And I imagine some of them will be things you don't particularly want to hear," she replied. "Now, since we're parked on Shore Road and neither of us ate a bite of our meal, why don't we get something to eat? My treat." Again, she leveled an unyielding look at him. "Or you can take me home, then sulk for the rest of the afternoon and complain that I bailed on you yet again."

She held her breath as she waited for him to make his choice. It seemed to take an eternity as he weighed the options.

"I suppose I could eat," he said grudgingly.

She resisted the temptation to reach over and ruffle his hair as she said, "You always could. You and Kevin were bottomless pits."

"We were growing boys," he countered as he got out and, to her surprise, came around and opened the car door for her. It was evidence, she thought, of Nell's stern emphasis on manners. It also demonstrated that no matter how badly Connor wanted to hate her, on some level he still had at least a tiny grain of respect left for the mother she'd been before the fateful day when she'd left Mick to save herself and turned all their lives upside down in the process.

Mick paced around the kitchen as Nell and Abby cleaned up after their dinner.

"I think I should go looking for them," he said for probably the tenth time since Connor had stormed off and Megan had gone after him.

"No!" Nell said emphatically. She and Abby had taken turns talking him out of doing anything rash.

"Mom needs to deal with Connor," Abby repeated. "If she's smart, she's probably somewhere in town feeding him a steak about now."

Mick paused. "You think they went to dinner? I could drive around, look for his car. Make sure no blood has been shed."

"No!" Abby said, regarding him with impatience. "Dad, you can't fix this. It's up to Mom."

"Some of what happened was my fault," he argued.

"A lot of it was," Nell agreed, "but that's not the point. This is between your son and his mother. You can sort out your issues with him later."

"Well, I can't just sit around here," he grumbled.

"I've never been any good at sitting on the sidelines and waiting."

"But this time that's exactly what you'll do," Nell said firmly. "Now grab a dish towel and dry some of those pots and pans."

Mick sighed and took a towel from Abby, who promptly announced she was going to get Trace and her girls and head for home. She nodded silently toward Nell and mouthed to him, "Talk to her."

Mick got the message. After Abby had gone, he put the last of the pans back in the cabinet and turned to his mother. "Ma, sit down."

She regarded him with a narrowed gaze. "Why?"

"Because you're the one person who hasn't said how you feel about Megan and me getting married again."

She looked him directly in the eye and said, "I'm happy for both of you. This has been in the wind for a long time now. I've had time to get used to the idea."

Though her words and tone were meant to be convincing, Mick didn't buy it. "You do know that our marriage isn't going to displace you, right? This has been your home for a long time now, and Megan and I both want you to stay right here."

She gave him a defiant look. "What if I want to

go back to my own cottage and get on with the life you two disrupted when you split up?"

Startled, Mick stared at her. "*Is* that what you want?"

She sighed softly. "I can't say for sure, but it holds a certain appeal. It's not as if I'd be at the ends of the earth. The cottage is within walking distance. And it's mine. I fixed it up exactly the way I wanted it when you built it. It's warm and cozy, which would be a nice change from rattling around in this big old place now that all your children are grown and have moved out."

Mick felt a deep sense of loss at the thought of his mother going off to live on her own. Still, he said, "It's your decision, Ma, as long as you know you're welcome here if you want to stay. This became your home the day you moved in here to help me with the kids. I dumped most of that responsibility on your shoulders because I couldn't cope. I'll owe you till the day I die."

"You don't owe me a thing. I did what was necessary," she insisted. "And I'm thinking you and Megan should have a fresh start without me underfoot. She probably has her own ideas about how she'd like the household to run."

"She'll more than likely be working, Ma. The house would continue to be your domain."

"Like some glorified housekeeper," she said with asperity, then held up a hand. "I didn't mean that to sound so harsh. I do know you both want me here, and I appreciate that. We have a couple of months to think about it. Maybe I'll go over to the cottage tomorrow and see how it's holding up. It could probably use a fresh coat of paint and airing out. No matter the care I've taken of it, a house suffers when it's not lived in."

"I'll come with you," Mick offered. "Anything you want done, I'll take care of it. And if you change your mind and decide to stay here, that's fine, too."

Her expression suddenly brightened, and a twinkle lit her eyes. "It might be nice to have my own place if I should have a gentleman caller."

Mick stared at her. "Excuse me?"

"You never know, young man. I'm old, but I'm not in my grave yet."

"Far from it," Mick said, shaking his head. He wondered if Nell O'Brien would ever stop surprising him. He had a hunch if she had her way, there might be a few more shocks in store.

* * *

Even though they'd managed to get through dinner, Megan wasn't deluding herself that anything between her and Connor was truly settled. Once again,
he'd resorted to the kind of civility that had fooled
all of them into believing he'd weathered the divorce
without scars. Now that she knew otherwise, she'd
be more attuned to the hostility that seethed just
beneath the surface. One dinner without fireworks
wasn't going to change that.

By the time Connor dropped her off at the house,
she was emotionally wrung out. Finding Mick pacing impatiently in the foyer did nothing to soothe her.

"It's about time," he muttered when she walked
inside. "Where's Connor?"

"On his way back to Baltimore," she said wearily.

"Why didn't he come inside?"

She lifted a brow. "So you could badger him?"

He frowned at her. "I wasn't going to badger him,
just tell him a few facts of life."

"Well, he doesn't need to hear anything more from
either one of us at the moment. He needs time to process what's happening. Once again, we've turned his
view of the world upside down."

"This isn't about him," Mick grumbled.

"Of course it is," Megan said. "What I did years ago had an impact on each one of our children. So did the way you chose to handle it—by running off to one job site after another. What I thought of as consideration for their feelings in letting them stay here in their home with you, they interpreted as me not caring at all. There were bound to be repercussions."

"I suppose," he said grudgingly. "I just hope Connor didn't try to talk you out of marrying me."

"Of course he did," she said, then touched Mick's cheek. "There's nothing he could say, though, that would change my mind, Mick. We might have to adjust the timetable a bit to allow time to bring him around, but in the end, we will get married."

He stopped pacing and stared. "Adjust the timetable? What the devil are you suggesting?"

"That New Year's Eve may be rushing things. I want everyone in the family not only to attend the ceremony, but to be happy for us, Mick. It won't feel right if they're not."

He faced her stubbornly. "We're getting married New Year's Eve, and that's that."

She frowned. "And there's no room for compromise, even if it's important to me?"

Apparently he heard the warning note in her voice, because he backed down at once. "I didn't say that."

"No, you just said it's your way, period. This isn't going to work, Mick, not if we can't work through things like this together."

He scowled unhappily, but eventually nodded. "Okay, fine, we'll talk about it. You want a drink?"

"Just some tea, I think."

"I'll fix it," he offered, then headed for the kitchen.

There was no one in this Irish household who couldn't brew a proper cup of tea. Mick placed a steaming pot before her within minutes, then sat down.

"Were you able to talk with Nell?" she asked, hoping to avoid another argument over Connor.

He nodded. "She thinks she might want to move to the cottage."

"Oh, dear," Megan said. "That's exactly what I was hoping to avoid."

"Don't fret too much. She seems to think it will improve her social life," Mick said, clearly disgruntled. "She said something about having privacy for her gentlemen callers. Since when does my mother have gentlemen callers, I'd like to know?"

Megan chuckled. "Maybe that's the point," she

suggested. "She doesn't want you to know about them and meddle the way you have in your children's lives."

He shuddered. "She's probably right. Knowing my mother is getting involved with some old codger is probably more information than I need to have."

"I think it would be sweet for her to have someone special in her life," Megan said thoughtfully. "Look at all the years she's sacrificed her own needs to take care of our family. It's her turn to find whatever happiness she can."

"I suppose. Now let's stop talking about my mother and Connor, and focus on us. How soon are you going to quit your job and move down here? Two weeks' notice ought to be enough, don't you think?"

"Not with a major show coming up at the gallery," she said. "Besides, if I want Phillip to consider opening an extension of his gallery here, then I have to handle this with care."

"You don't need his backing," Mick argued. "I'll bankroll your gallery."

"It's very generous of you to want to do that," Megan said, "but I just finished telling Connor that I wasn't marrying you for your money. How will it look to him if you pour thousands of dollars into my new business? No, Mick. I have to make this come together on my own."

"How?" he asked, his skepticism plain...and highly annoying.

"That's my problem now, isn't it?"

"Is this the way it's going to be from here on out?" he demanded. "You refusing to accept any kind of help from me? I want to do things for you, Megan. It makes me happy."

"Then buy me a bouquet of flowers from time to time, or take me out for a romantic dinner. I don't need lavish gestures for you to prove how much you love me."

Mick shook his head. "You are the most contrary woman I've ever known. What kind of person turns down help from someone who loves them?"

"One who needs to maintain some independence," she responded candidly.

"Why, so you can turn right around and leave me again?"

"No, so there will never be a question in your mind that I'm with you because I love you, not because of what you can do for me."

"That's Connor talking," he said. "I won't have

him meddling in our relationship or making you question the way every little thing we do might look to him."

"It's not about Connor," she insisted. "It's about me, Mick. I've learned to stand on my own two feet. I'm not the naive, dependent girl who expected you to dance attendance and make my life complete. If it's going to work between us, we have to be equals."

"So if I decide on impulse to give you a car, you have to turn right around and buy something for me?" he asked.

"That might be exaggerating just a bit," she said dryly.

"Well, I should hope so, because it sounds ridiculous. If I'm your husband and I decide on a whim to give you something, what happened to accepting it graciously?"

"Mick, this isn't about cars or jewelry or impulsive gestures."

"Then explain it to me."

Megan wasn't sure she could. She just knew that gifts per se weren't the problem. It was all the strings implied. And if she wasn't careful, those strings were going to bind them together for all the wrong reasons.

And their marriage wouldn't stand a chance.

* * *

Mick had been thoroughly frustrated by his conversation with Megan the night before. He was still
stewing over it on Monday morning after he'd driven
her to Baltimore to the airport. He knew Connor was
behind her attitude, no matter how much she'd tried
to deny it. He also knew he needed to settle a thing
or two with his younger son.

He pulled out his cell phone and called Connor at
the office. "Take a break," he ordered without pre-
amble. "I'll meet you at the coffee shop on the corner in ten minutes."

"I can't. I have an appointment with a new client
in an hour."

"This won't take long," Mick said grimly. "I'll talk
and you can listen."

Of course, that was an optimistic outlook. Connor
had never once suffered a lecture in silence. Those
strong opinions of his were bound to surface. Still,
Mick wanted to clear the air and make a few things
plain. His son might be a grown man, but Mick still
ran the family. He was due a little respect of his own.

Connor was already waiting at a table with two
cups of coffee by the time Mick had found a parking place and walked the two blocks to the crowded

little café. "Parking in this city is a nuisance," he grumbled as he sat.

"Is that why you wanted to see me," Connor inquired, "to complain about the parking in downtown Baltimore?"

Mick frowned at the sarcasm. "You know perfectly well it's not. We need to discuss the wedding."

Connor looked as if he was ready to launch into another diatribe, so Mick cut him off before he could get started.

"You will not interfere," Mick told him flatly. "You don't have to approve of it. You don't have to like it. But you will stay out of it." He leveled a hard look into his son's eyes. "And you will show up for the ceremony with a smile on your face. Is that understood?"

Connor gave him a knowing look. "Mom's talking about postponing, isn't she?"

"That's not an option," Mick said forcefully.

"But I got to her yesterday and now she's having second thoughts," Connor said with a triumphant note. "Good for her."

Mick regarded him with sorrow. "Do you care nothing for my feelings?"

Connor looked shocked by the question. "Of

course I do! Dad, can't you see that I'm trying to protect you? You've gotten all caught up in sentiment. You're not thinking clearly."

Mick was none too pleased by his son's determination to interfere, to say nothing of his confidence that only he knew what was best for his parents. "Connor, I'm a grown man. I don't need looking after, no matter how well-intentioned it might be. I love your mother. I always have. God's seen fit to give me a second chance with her, and I won't let you or anyone else take that away from us."

"She'll break your heart again," Connor predicted.

"I don't believe that, but if it happens, so be it."

"You can't mean that. The last time she left, it almost destroyed you. It almost ruined our entire family."

"I thought Bree was the one in the family with a flair for drama," Mick chided. "What happened was devastating for all of us, no question about it. But look at Abby, Bree and Kevin today. They're all happily married. Jess has a thriving business she loves. And even you have found your life's work. We're more tight-knit as a family than we have been in years."

"All of that's in spite of Mom, not because of her."

"Maybe so, but we can hardly claim that what she did ruined our lives. It shaped us, to be sure. It changed her, as well—for the better, I think. She's stronger and more independent."

"You almost sound as if you approve of that," Connor said.

"Well, of course I do. I made your mother very unhappy. I wasn't the partner she needed. I think we're a better match today than we were back then."

"Just how long do you think it will take before this independent streak of hers gets on your nerves?" Connor asked.

Mick chuckled. "It already has. More than once, in fact. That doesn't mean it's not for the best. None of this is your worry, son. All we need from you is your blessing, even if you disagree with the choice we're making."

Looking genuinely distressed, Connor shook his head. "I can't do it, Dad. Not when this marriage has disaster written all over it. I've already told Mom I'm going to draw up a prenuptial agreement."

"You did what?" Mick was aghast. "You most certainly will not. I don't believe in starting a marriage trying to figure out how it will end."

"It's commonplace for someone in your position," Connor insisted.

"No!" Mick said, slamming his fist on the table.

Connor didn't bend. "Dad, I'll do whatever I can to protect you, whether you want me to or not."

Mick bristled at his unrelenting attitude. "Then you'll stay away," he ordered. "From this moment on, you'll stay away."

"Stay away?" Connor repeated, his expression incredulous.

"From Chesapeake Shores, from our house," Mick said, his gaze unyielding.

"I'm not welcome in my own home?" Connor said, looking shaken.

"Not until you can see your way clear to treat your mother with the respect she deserves and can accept our marriage."

Connor's expression hardened. "Then I guess it will be a cold day in hell before I set foot in Chesapeake Shores again."

Even as he spoke, he stood up. He cast one last bleak look at Mick, then, his back stiff with pride, he walked away, never once looking back.

As he went, Mick felt his heart break. He also

knew that when Megan learned of this—and she no doubt would—she might never forgive him for causing a possibly irreparable rift with their son.

3

For the next week Mick left the house before dawn and didn't return until well after dusk. If he'd been able to think of a reason to leave town for business, he'd have been on the first flight out of Baltimore, but lately his out-of-state projects were all running smoothly under the direction of his second-in-command, Jaime Alvarez. Mick wouldn't undermine Jaime by showing up unannounced. Besides, he had plenty of work nearby with his Habitat for Humanity projects to send him home exhausted at the end of the day.

He'd been avoiding Megan's calls, as well. He knew that sooner or later she was going to catch up with him and he'd have to tell her about Connor, but he wasn't quite ready for that conversation.

When he walked into the kitchen on Friday night and found both Abby and Nell sitting at the table, he knew his time for avoiding this latest mess was over.

"Your dinner's in the oven, probably all dried out," Nell commented without a hint of apology. "Serves you right for not coming home on time and not calling."

"Sorry, Ma," he said, then glanced at Abby and noted her sour expression. "Everything okay with you?"

"I think you know it's not," she said icily.

"You've spoken to your brother, then?" he said, resigned.

Abby regarded him critically. "Dad, what were you thinking? You banished Connor. I know he's stubborn and exasperating, but he's family."

"Apparently he's also a tattletale," Mick said, though he knew that was hardly the point. "I didn't expect him to go running to his big sister whining about it."

"What *did* you expect?" Nell inquired. "That he'd

take this punishment of yours quietly? That's not in his makeup. Surely you know him well enough to know that."

"I was hoping to shake him up," Mick said with a shrug. "I wanted him to see how important my marriage to his mother is to me. I wanted him to accept it and get on board."

"Well, I'd say your approach backfired," Nell said. "He's angrier than ever."

"Does Mom know about this?" Abby asked.

"Of course not," Nell answered for him. She directed an accusing look his way as she plunked his reheated food in front of him. "Otherwise he wouldn't be avoiding her calls."

"I'm not avoiding Megan," he said, though of course he was. "I've been busy."

"Interesting that being overwhelmed with work hasn't kept you from speaking to her half a dozen times a day for the past few months," Nell noted. "Did you think she wouldn't notice that you haven't spoken all week? She's been calling here for days now looking for answers. Did you expect me to lie for you?"

Mick stared at his mother in dismay. "You didn't tell her what's going on, did you?"

"It's not up to me," Nell replied. "You do your own dirty work."

"I'll call her tonight," he promised, cutting into the overcooked, dried-up piece of beef on his plate. Not even his mother's excellent gravy could save it. He pushed the plate aside.

"And say what?" Abby wanted to know. "Are you going to tell her about Connor?"

"For all I know he's blabbed to her himself," he grumbled.

"If he were speaking to her, he might have, but I doubt he broke silence to fill her in on this," Abby said. "Dad, you need to fix this before Mom finds out. If she hears about you telling Connor to stay away from his own home, you know she'll postpone the wedding until it's resolved."

Mick grimaced. "That's what I was trying to avoid when I went to see him. I wanted peace."

"And instead you've made it worse," Nell said. "Mick, you've always had the tact of a bulldozer. And Connor's more like you than anyone else in the family. You should have known better."

He scowled at the two women. "Are you going to sit here berating me, or are you going to help me straighten this out before Megan gets wind of it? Do either one of you actually have any helpful suggestions?"

"You could start by calling Connor and apologizing. Tell him you didn't mean it," Abby suggested.

"But I meant every word," Mick argued stubbornly. "He's the one who needs to change his attitude."

"You're not going to win him over by banishing him," Nell said. "That's not a tactic to win anyone's heart. All it tells him is that you're choosing his mother over him."

"Well, what would you have me do?" he asked testily. "Cave in and tell him it's just fine if he wants to do his best to ruin the wedding?"

"Of course not," Abby said. "But he needs to spend more time here, not less, and he and Mom need to be thrown together as much as possible. She'll win him over. It may not happen on your timetable, but it will happen."

"I'm not postponing this wedding," Mick insisted, his jaw set.

"If Mom finds out about this, you may not have a choice," Abby said realistically. "She's determined that this family will be united and at peace before the ceremony takes place."

"Well, I can't be expected to work miracles, now can I?" Mick grumbled and threw down his napkin.

Nell put her hand on his. "No, but 'tis the season of them. Perhaps there's one waiting in the wings."

Mick's faith was as strong as any man's most of the time. Right this second, though, he doubted there was a miracle on tap that could possibly fix this mess he'd made.

Megan knew there was something seriously wrong in Chesapeake Shores. Even if Mick hadn't been clearly avoiding her, it was plain in Nell's voice and in Abby's. No matter how hard she'd tried, though, she hadn't been able to get the truth out of either one of them.

"I can't get down there this weekend to see for myself," she complained to Abby. "Keeping me in the dark is just making me imagine all sorts of things. Is it the baby? Has Bree been having problems with her pregnancy?"

"Bree is fine," Abby assured her. "Healthy as a horse, according to the doctor. She seems to have more energy than ever. She's been getting ready for the children's Christmas play at her theater. I went to a rehearsal the other night and the kids are absolutely precious, Mom. Wait till you see them."

"I'm sure they are," Megan said distractedly. "What about Jess? Is she okay? The inn hasn't suffered another financial setback, has it?"

"Business at the inn is booming. Jess is doing a fantastic job. Bookings for the holidays are strong."

"Kevin and Shanna, they're okay? Henry's biological father isn't making trouble about the adoption, is he?"

"Mother, I can't speak for every single person in Chesapeake Shores, but all of the O'Briens are just fine," Abby said, apparently losing patience with Megan's persistent, probing questions. "Now I need to go. I promised Carrie and Caitlyn I'd take them into town to see the decorations today. Santa's going to be at Ethel's, too. They've already put on their coats and gloves. I need to get them out of the house before they roast or burst with excitement."

"Well, if you happen to cross paths with your father, tell him that if I don't hear from him by the end of the day, the wedding's off," she said, meaning it.

Just because Abby had uttered a bunch of reassuring platitudes didn't make Megan believe her. Being kept in the dark about something was unacceptable, and she knew without a doubt that Mick was somehow all mixed up in this pact of silence.

"You don't mean that," Abby said, sounding dismayed.

"Actually I do," she said firmly. "I will not turn my life upside down to come back there, if this is the way I can expect to be treated. I feel like an outsider, instead of a member of this family. You're all keeping secrets from me, and I want you to know I don't like it."

"I'm not the one who needs to hear that," Abby protested.

"Well, of course you aren't," Megan said impatiently. "If I could get your father on the phone for two minutes, I'd tell him that myself. Since I can't, you'll just have to be the messenger."

"Mom, I really don't want to get caught in the middle," Abby said, a pleading note in her voice.

"Oh, fiddlesticks. You've planted yourself in the middle for quite some time now. You should be used to the role."

Abby sighed. "I love you, Mom."

"And I love you. It's my feelings for your father I'm starting to question. Give the girls huge hugs for me, okay?"

"Will do," Abby promised.

Megan let her go, then hung up, even more frustrated than she'd been when she made the call. She looked up and found her boss regarding her worriedly.

"Megan, are you absolutely certain that moving back to Chesapeake Shores and marrying Mick is what you want?" Phillip Margolin asked. "If Mick is already shutting you out, it seems to me that's not a good sign."

She met his concerned gaze. "Right this second, I'm not sure about anything," she admitted.

"Then stay," he urged. "You know you're valued here. You've made a wonderful life for yourself in New York."

"I have," she conceded. "But my family's there. I don't want to live the rest of my life apart from them."

"Even though Mick is clearly exasperating you?"

She smiled. Only a lifelong confirmed bachelor could ask a question like that. "That's what he does, but I can't seem to make myself stop loving him just the same."

From the moment she'd told Phillip of her plans, he'd tried to be supportive, but it was plain he wasn't above using this to keep her right where she was. Letting her go was going to disrupt the smooth running of his gallery. Still, his tone resigned, he asked, "Do you want to go down there now and find out for yourself what's going on?"

She considered the offer, then shook her head. "We have the opening next week. Whatever's going on in Chesapeake Shores can wait until I go there for Thanksgiving."

"Are you certain? Will you be able to focus if you're worrying about your family?"

"I've always worried about my family," she reminded him. "And I've never lost focus yet."

That didn't mean the next two weeks wouldn't be a struggle, but perhaps it was just as well not to be anywhere near Mick when he seemed intent on infuriating her.

Mick sat at a table in the coffee area of Shanna's bookstore, relieved to be around family who apparently had no idea about what was going on or about the secret he was keeping from Megan. He'd found a new mystery by his favorite author, poured himself a steaming cup of coffee and was contentedly reading when Davy and Henry suddenly appeared.

Davy immediately climbed into his lap, while Henry stood shyly by. Mick brightened at the sight of them.

"Well, now, where did the two of you come from?" he asked as Davy dug in Mick's pocket and retrieved two wrapped candies, then handed one to Henry.

"We were looking at the store windows with Aunt Abby, Carrie and Caitlyn," Henry said.

"I saw Santa," Davy announced excitedly. "He was at Ethel's. He promised he's going to bring lots and lots of presents for Henry and me."

"Is that so?" Mick said. "Have you sent him a list?"

Davy shook his head. "I told him what I want."

"Well, it never hurts for Santa to have it in writing," Mick said. He noticed that Henry looked skeptical and gathered that he'd already stopped believing. Still, he clearly didn't intend to ruin it for his younger brother.

"Maybe Mommy will help me make one," Davy said, a worried frown puckering his brow. "Henry can write his own. He knows how."

"I know. He's a very smart young man," Mick said, giving the older boy a wink. "Why wait, though? If you ask your mother for a piece of paper, maybe I can help you now."

Davy's eyes immediately brightened. "Really?"

"Sure. I've written many a letter to Santa over the years."

After Davy had run off, Mick beckoned for Henry to come closer. "Are you so sure Santa doesn't exist?"

"I knew better when I was seven," he said sadly. "I told him all I wanted was for my daddy to get better, but he hasn't. He's still sick. He can't take care of me anymore."

Henry's biological father was an alcoholic whose liver had been severely damaged by the disease. That's why Shanna, who'd only briefly been his stepmother, had been given custody after negotiating the arrangement with Henry's father and grandparents. Now Kevin had legally adopted him, as well. At the same time Shanna had formally adopted Davy, whose biological mom had died while serving in Iraq. They were the ultimate modern family, pieced together by love.

"But your dad still loves you very much," Mick assured Henry. "That's why he's agreed to let you be with Shanna and Kevin, so you'll have the kind of life you deserve. Maybe that's the gift that Santa meant for you—the gift of a new family, plus your old one. You're very lucky to have so many people who love you."

Henry pondered that in the serious little way he had, then nodded. "I suppose."

"So maybe Santa would bring you something special this Christmas if he knew you still believed in him. Why not get a piece of paper and take a chance?" Mick coaxed.

"I guess it wouldn't hurt to try," Henry said, his eyes suddenly brimming with hope.

"Go then and bring your paper back here. I'll see that Santa gets your letter and Davy's."

"Thanks, Grandpa Mick."

As he scampered off, Abby settled into the chair opposite him.

"So much for finding a refuge in here," he muttered with a resigned sigh.

"I have a message from Mom," she said.

Mick's stomach knotted with dread. "Oh?"

"She says if she doesn't hear from you very, very soon, the wedding's off."

"Now, what kind of message is that to be sending through you?" Mick blustered.

"The kind sent by a frustrated woman who's losing patience," Abby assessed. "Now that I've delivered it, I'm taking the girls next door for lunch. You're welcome to join us."

"I have letters to Santa to oversee," he said. "And then I've a phone call to make."

She patted his hand. "Good decision."

Mick wondered about that, because right this second he had absolutely no idea what he was going to say to Megan that wouldn't wind up with her not just postponing their wedding, but canceling it.

Mick had tucked the boys' letters to Santa into his pocket and sent them off for naps when Kevin appeared. Apparently he was taking over for his wife while she dealt with settling the boys upstairs in the apartment where she'd lived before marrying Kevin. She'd kept it so the kids could be cared for close by while she worked in the store.

"So, Dad, what's going on between you and Connor?" Kevin asked point-blank, studying him intently.

"Who says there's anything going on?" Mick replied defensively. "You saw the way he stormed out of the house. He's not happy about your mother and me remarrying."

"I know that, but when I spoke to him the other day and suggested he come down and go fishing today, he mumbled some kind of ridiculous excuse that didn't make a bit of sense. I reminded him I needed his help to get the boat ready for the lighted boat parade the first weekend in December, and he blew that off, too."

"Maybe he's busy," Mick suggested. "He's working hard to make partner at the law firm, and he probably spends a lot of his spare time with that woman he's been seeing."

Kevin looked surprised. "You know about Heather?"

Mick brightened. "Is that her name?"

Kevin frowned at him. "You were just taking a stab in the dark, weren't you, you sneaky old man? You had no idea he was dating anyone."

"He's a good-looking, successful young man. I never thought he was living the life of a monk."

"But you didn't know about any specific woman," Kevin persisted.

"Nope," Mick confirmed with a satisfied grin. "So, how serious is it?"

"Ask Connor." Kevin's expression turned sly. "Or aren't the two of you speaking?"

"Now who's resorting to guesswork?"

"I wouldn't need to, if either one of you would give me a straight answer. Dad, if marrying Mom is going to come between you and Connor, maybe you should rethink it."

"You'd have me put my life on hold because any one of you can't be an adult and accept that I know exactly what I'm doing?" Mick asked incredulously.

"Look, Mom and I are getting along okay now, but I've had time to reconcile the perspective I used to have with the realities of what actually happened back then," Kevin said, his tone reasonable. "Connor's not had enough time, plus he's even more hard-headed than you or I on our bad days. Why not have a spring wedding? Mom can walk along the pathway that's lined with all those lilies of the valley she planted. It'll be beautiful."

"I am not waiting until spring just so your brother can make peace with this. If he knows he has that kind of power over the two of us, he'll find some other way to force us to postpone that date. Years could go by while he manipulates the situation. In case you haven't noticed, neither your mother or I are getting any younger."

"I wouldn't suggest you use Mom's advancing age as an excuse for pressing ahead with a New Year's Eve wedding," Kevin said with a grin.

Mick scowled at him. "Of course not. Do you think I'm crazy?"

"Sometimes you do say things without thinking through the consequences," Kevin said. "Something tells me that's what happened with Connor." He studied Mick intently. "Is that it, Dad? Did you back him into a corner?"

"We'll work it out," Mick said. "That's what O'Briens do. We work things out."

"Unless those *things* you're talking about happen to be between you and Uncle Jeff or you and Uncle Thomas," Kevin said knowingly. "How many years have the three of you been at odds? The only thing you and Thomas have managed to agree on is that Shanna and I belong together."

"Whole different story," Mick insisted. He heard the bell over the store's front door ring, spotted Daisy Monroe coming inside with her pet poodle clutched in her arms and seized on the excuse. "You have a customer. Take care of her. I'm going home."

The whole conversation with Kevin had left him more disgruntled than ever. He was in no mood to call Megan, but judging from the message she'd sent via Abby, he didn't have a choice. Maybe he could bluster his way through it.

He walked down to Shore Road, found an unoccupied bench facing the bay where cell phone reception would be good, then placed the call.

"Meggie, my love, how are you?" he said exuberantly when she answered.

"I was better before you started avoiding me," she said, her tone testy. "What's going on, Mick? Don't you dare lie to me and tell me it's nothing."

"Just a little glitch," he claimed. "Nothing for you to worry about."

"Mick O'Brien!"

"I'm telling you everything's going to work out. Don't you have that big show at the gallery this week? Tell me about that. Is everything coming together? I'm planning on flying up, you know."

"Do not change the subject on me," she said. "I want to know what's going on. I'm not some outsider. Nor do I need to be protected from things."

"Is this another of those partnership things you keep bringing up?"

"Yes, that's exactly what it is," she told him. "If there is anything going on with our family, then I need to be kept in the loop."

Mick debated continuing with further evasiveness, but he could tell from her tone that she was losing patience. Sooner or later she'd learn the truth. She might as well hear it from him. At least he could put the best possible spin on it, assuming he could come up with one.

"I stopped by to see Connor the other day," he admitted eventually. "After I dropped you at the airport, in fact."

"And the two of you fought," she guessed at once. "Oh, Mick, why couldn't you just leave it alone? I warned you he needed more time."

"With a wedding in a couple of months, time is exactly what we don't have. I decided to move things along."

"What happened?"

"I just told you. I went to see our son," he said defensively.

"And?"

"I couldn't make him see reason," he admitted.

"In other words, he's still opposed to our marriage."

"You could say that."

"Well, thank goodness Thanksgiving is right around the corner. We'll all be together then. If we can get Connor to come for the whole holiday weekend, it'll give me more time to get through to him. And you can use the time to apologize for whatever you said."

"I don't owe him an apology," Mick said indignantly. "He's the one who ought to be apologizing for trying to interfere in our plans. He told me about that ridiculous prenuptial agreement he wants us to sign. I told him I wasn't interested."

Megan fell silent. Mick was tempted to fill the void, but he knew perfectly well that the odds were he'd only make matters worse.

"Mick, how bad did things get between you and Connor?" Megan asked eventually, her voice filled with trepidation.

"He said some things," Mick admitted. "I said some things. It might have gotten a little heated."

Megan groaned. "I know what that means. It means it all got wildly out of hand."

"It wasn't all my fault," he insisted.

"Maybe not, but it's up to you to make it right," she told him emphatically. "I mean it, Mick. Talk to Connor and settle this."

"It's already settled," he said stubbornly.

"Meaning you've dug in your heels and so has he," she said wearily. "Okay, I'll call him and try to smooth things over. Maybe we can bond over how infuriating we both find you to be."

"No," he said hurriedly. "Leave it alone, Megan. I insist that you stay out of it."

"Excuse me?" she said, her voice soft and deadly calm.

"I didn't mean to make it sound like an order," he said, scrambling to soothe her ruffled feathers. "It's just that I need to deal with Connor."

"Then do it," she said direly. "Call me and let me know how it goes."

"Will do," he said as if it were going to be a quick fix.

When she'd hung up, Mick breathed a sigh of relief. As bad as the conversation had been, somehow he'd managed to avoid telling her that he'd banished Connor from Chesapeake Shores. Which meant he either had to get his son home for Thanksgiving or prepare to cancel his plans for a wedding on New Year's Eve.

4

It was two days before Thanksgiving before Megan came back to Chesapeake Shores. Though there had been precious little time for anything other than preparations for their big show opening, she'd managed to have at least a few conversations with Phillip about starting a gallery of her own. She had pages of notes she wanted to go over during the long holiday weekend. He'd given her a lot of things to think about.

Though Phillip was willing to consider a branch of his Upper East Side gallery, they'd both agreed she might be happier with a business over which she had total control. Phillip would act as her mentor and would help her to arrange shows with some of his regular artists, most of whom she'd come to know well over the years. Many would be happy to have a new outlet for their work.

Megan had enough savings to get things in motion, but she would need additional capital to operate for the first year. She planned to see Lawrence Riley—her son-in-law Trace's father—at the bank over the next couple of days to discuss a small business loan. She was optimistic that her experience in New York, combined with the business plan she'd devised with Phillip's help, would be enough to impress the bank president.

Despite her determination to do all of this on her own, she was realistic enough to understand that her remarriage to Mick would come into play. Somehow, though, she would find a way to show Lawrence Riley and everyone else here in town that she might be Mrs. Mick O'Brien once more, but she nevertheless had her own separate and independent life. It would probably be difficult for some people to adjust to that idea, but she wanted to start that process now.

Beyond her business plans, there were a million and one details to finalize even for the small family wedding that she and Mick envisioned. Not the least of the things she hoped to accomplish was building on the overture she'd made to Connor on her last visit.

It was so important to her that all of the children be comfortable with her coming back to town once again as Mick's wife. That was going to be even trickier, she feared, than teaching their neighbors to view her in a new way, especially after whatever had happened between Connor and Mick. She still needed to get to the bottom of that. Something told her she knew only part of the story. Even during Mick's quick visit to New York the previous week, he'd remained stubbornly evasive about the details.

When she arrived Tuesday morning, she insisted Mick drop her off on Main Street. "Bree and I can talk about the flowers for the wedding. Then I want to stop by the bank to see Lawrence."

Mick frowned. "Why would you need to see him?"

"If I'm going to open that art gallery we talked about, I'll need to arrange for a loan."

"Nonsense," Mick said at once. "I've already told you that I'll give you whatever money you need."

She scowled at him. "And then it won't be my business, will it? No, Mick. We've talked about this. I need to do this on my own. I have a solid business plan."

To her annoyance, he looked skeptical. "Maybe you should run it by me first. I have a lot of experience dealing with Lawrence. I know the kind of questions he's likely to ask."

"Absolutely not!" she said stubbornly, then backed down at his hurt expression. "It's not that I don't want you to see the business plan, Mick. I'm sure your insight would be very helpful, but I just feel this is something I have to handle on my own."

"Why?"

"To prove to everyone that I'm my own person now."

"Well, before you go dashing off to the bank, you need to come with me," he said, looking thoroughly disgruntled. Instead of parking on Main Street as she'd requested, he drove around the corner to Shore Road. At the end of the block, he pulled into a spot in front of an empty corner storefront. Large windows faced both Shore Road and Seagull Lane, while the door opened at an angle to both streets. It was a prime location, no question about it, and more square footage than she'd dreamed of having.

"I was planning on giving you this as a wedding present," Mick said. "But I can't very well have you going off to get a loan from the bank to lease something else in the meantime."

Megan turned to him, mouth agape. "You leased this?"

"I bought it," he corrected. "Well, truthfully, I already owned it. Jeff and I still own all the property in the business district. He manages the leases. I've put the lease for this in your name for as long as you want it."

"Mick, I can't afford the rent on a property this size," Megan protested. "It's bound to cost a fortune."

"It's yours for a dollar a year," he said, his jaw set stubbornly. "The lease is already drawn up and signed."

The generosity of the gesture brought tears to Megan's eyes, but she shook her head. "Mick, you know I can't accept this. I told Connor I wasn't marrying you for your money, that I intended to stand on my own two feet. Accepting a free rental property is the same as taking money from you." She shook her head. "I just can't do it."

"Leave Connor out of this. I want to do this for you," he said. "I know you value your independence, but a husband ought to be able to do something nice for his wife. Opening this gallery means a lot to you, and I want to be some small part of that. Bree let me do the finishing construction on her flower shop, and Jess allowed me to do a few small things for her at the inn. She even accepted that fancy stove her chef wanted. Think of this the same way, as my contribution to getting your business up and running."

Reluctantly, Megan nodded. Arguing further not only seemed ungrateful, but pointless. "It's an amazing gift, Mick. Thank you." Shoving aside her reservations, she regarded him eagerly. "Can we go inside? What was here before? I can't recall that I was ever in this space."

He shook his head. "I doubt you were. It sold sunglasses, beach floats, boogie boards, bathing suits and some sporting equipment. Probably would have gone over in Ocean City, but with Ethel's selling a lot of the same things for a whole lot less money, it didn't stand a chance. Jeff tried to warn the owners, but they were a couple of young guys with big ideas and a bankroll from their fathers. Couldn't tell them a thing. They barely covered their overhead. Lasted through the summer, then threw in the towel after Labor Day."

"Well, their loss is my gain," Megan said as she waited for Mick to open the door.

Once inside, Megan knew she couldn't possibly change her mind and say no. The property was ideal. It was filled with natural light. The walls had already been painted in the same neutral tone as the gallery in New York.

"You've had it painted?" she asked, sniffing the scent of fresh paint in the air.

Mick nodded. "I called Phillip and asked him what color he recommended. That's as far as I've gone, though," he assured her. "I haven't done anything to upgrade the lighting yet, because I thought you'd want to have a say in that."

Megan pressed a kiss to his cheek. "You really are amazing."

He studied her worriedly. "You're not mad at me for being presumptuous?"

"How can I be?" she said. "This is an incredible space, and the location couldn't be more perfect."

But she did wonder if she'd just set a dangerous

precedent. Mick had always been the kind of man who, in his zeal to make his family happy, had a way of taking over. Give him an inch, he took not just the proverbial mile, but most of the county. It was going to take every bit of strength she possessed to stand up to him.

After leaving Mick, Megan walked over to the bank. She was aware when she stepped into the lobby that several of the people who'd worked there for years were giving her surreptitious looks, but no one actually met her gaze as she walked over to Lawrence Riley's longtime secretary, a woman with whom she'd once had at least a casual friendship.

"Hello, Mariah," she said quietly. "Is Lawrence available?"

Mariah hesitated just long enough to indicate that she, like many others, hadn't forgotten that Megan had walked out on the town's most prominent citizen and left five children behind. Her disapproval obviously hadn't lessened over time.

"Did you have an appointment?" Mariah asked coldly. "His calendar's pretty jammed today."

"I'm sure it is, but if he could spare a few minutes, I'd really appreciate it."

With obvious reluctance, Mariah picked up her phone. Before dialing, she asked, "Can I tell him what it's about?"

"I'm hoping to start a business here in town. I'd like to discuss a small business loan."

For an instant Mariah's mouth gaped, then she turned away and mumbled something into the phone. When she turned back, she said, "He'll see you now." There was no mistaking how unhappy she was about that.

"Thanks, Mariah," Megan said, then ventured a smile. "It's good to see you. You're looking well."

She walked away quickly so the other woman wouldn't be forced to utter a reply she didn't mean.

Lawrence was standing when she reached his office. "Megan," he said, his welcome far more jovial than Mariah's had been. "I heard you might be returning to town. It's all Abby's been able to talk about lately. Of course, my wife and I aren't so sure how we feel about having to share Carrie and Caitlyn with their Grandma Megan. We love those little girls as if they were our own grandchildren."

Megan smiled. "They're wonderful, aren't they? I think they have plenty of energy and affection to satisfy all of us."

"True enough," he said. "I understand there are wedding plans afoot. Trace mentioned something about New Year's Eve."

"If all goes well, yes," she said.

He gestured toward a chair. "Sit down. Tell me what I can do for you."

"I'm hoping you'll approve a small business loan," she said, then withdrew her business plan from her briefcase and handed it to him. "All of the facts and figures are in there, along with an outline of my experience in New York. You'll see that I'm more than qualified to run an art gallery, that I have numerous connections to the New York art world. I can make a success of this, Lawrence."

"What's Mick's involvement going to be?" he asked bluntly.

"Financially, none," she said firmly.

Lawrence looked startled. Before he could express his obvious reservations, Megan held up a hand.

"However," she said, "he did make me a generous gift of a long-term lease on a property on Shore Road for a dollar a year. I just learned of that this morning, so the amount in my plan set aside for rent can be eliminated or devoted to expanding my inventory. Since overhead can kill a business that's just starting out, this has the potential to make a tremendous difference in how quickly I can turn a profit."

"I see," Lawrence said, nodding approvingly. "You know I don't make decisions like this alone, Megan, but I will take this before the loan committee next week. I'll get back to you after that meeting. Of course, it would be a sure thing if Mick were going to be involved...." His voice trailed off.

"But he won't be," she repeated emphatically. "This application should stand on its own merits, Lawrence. I don't want to mislead anyone by having them believe Mick is even a silent partner."

He stood then, calling an obvious end to the meeting. "I have to say I'm impressed with your business acumen. I'll do my best on your behalf, Megan. Once I've looked this plan of yours over more carefully, if I see any obvious red flags that need to be addressed, I'll contact you before the meeting next week."

"Thank you for seeing me, Lawrence, especially at the last minute."

"Of course. We're practically family, after all. Your daughter's made my son very happy."

Megan smiled. "And vice versa. Abby couldn't have found a better man for herself or a better stepfather for the twins."

"I just wish they'd hurry up and make me a grand-father again," he grumbled as he walked with her through the lobby. "They don't seem to be in any hurry, though."

"I know what you mean. I've had to learn to keep my mouth shut about things like that."

Megan said goodbye again at the door, pulled on her coat and stepped outside. Only after she'd walked down the block did she finally start to relax. She was pretty much oblivious to her surroundings when Bree stepped out of Flowers on Main and snagged her arm.

"Mom, were you just going to walk on by without stopping?" she asked.

"Oh, sweetie, I wasn't even paying attention to where I was," she said, then stood back to take a look at her daughter. "You're showing! When I was here before, you barely had a baby bump at all."

Bree grinned and put a protective hand on her rounded stomach. "I know. Isn't it amazing?" she said excitedly. "It's finally starting to seem real to me. I think Jake's still in shock. He just sits and stares at my belly as if it's growing right before his eyes."

"Your father was the same way when I was preg-nant for the first time with Abby," Megan confided. "It was almost impossible to keep him from pointing out my expanding waistline to strangers on the street."

"Do you have time to come in for a minute?" Bree asked. "We can talk about flowers for the wedding."

"Actually I'd planned to do that today. Then I got distracted," Megan said, following Bree inside. Jake's teenage niece Jenny was working at the cash register. Megan greeted her with a hug, then followed Bree into the back room. The mingling of so many flowery scents could have been overwhelming, but Megan breathed it in with delight.

"So, why were you so distracted?" Bree asked.

Megan described her meeting with Lawrence. "I couldn't tell if he was truly impressed with my plan or just placating me so he could leave it to the committee to turn me down."

"He won't turn you down, Mom. He wouldn't dare. Dad would raise a huge ruckus."

"I don't want a loan just because your father might get upset if it's denied."

"Mom, if you want this business, take the loan however you get it," Bree advised. "I'm sure Dad's the reason the bank okayed my loan and Jess's initially, even though he didn't cosign either one of them. After that one little blip at the inn, both loans have turned out to be very good investments. O'Briens are a safe bet and Lawrence knows it. As for the kind of things Dad does behind the scenes, I had to learn to turn a blind eye after he got the town to go along with my plans for a regional theater on part of the land in the park."

"I hope you're right," Megan said, her earlier confidence slipping despite Bree's reassuring words.

"Let's talk flowers," Bree said. "That will get your mind off of the meeting at the bank. Do you know what you want?"

For the next hour, they pored over Bree's portfolio of the weddings she'd done, as well as pictures of other floral arrangements. Megan was overwhelmed.

"I was thinking of something much simpler," she admitted. "Not that I don't want to give you a huge amount of business, but this wedding is going to be small and quiet. Do you mind if I think about it a little more?"

"Of course not. I actually have a couple of ideas for very simple bouquets that you might like. Maybe I'll make them up, so you can get a better idea if they're closer to what you pictured."

"Would you mind?" Megan asked, pleased.

"Of course not. If we're not swamped on Friday

with all of those Christmas sale shoppers wandering around town, I'll do it then," Bree promised. "Stop by sometime in the afternoon."

"Would you like an extra pair of hands in the morning in case it is busy?" Megan asked. "You shouldn't be on your feet too much."

"I have it covered," Bree assured her. She met Megan's gaze. "Mom, in case I didn't make it clear when you and Dad announced your plans, I am really happy for you. I'm especially glad you'll be here when the baby comes."

Her eyes misty, Megan pulled her daughter into an embrace. "Me, too, sweetie. Me, too."

In fact, that was just one of the many reasons she could hardly wait to come home again.

Mick walked into the bank right after he saw Megan leave. He acknowledged Mariah, but walked straight past her and into Lawrence's office. The banker regarded him with amusement.

"I wondered how long it would take before you showed up," he said. "You've never been able to leave well enough alone when it comes to your family."

"Have you?" Mick retorted, thinking of Lawrence's efforts to coerce Trace into taking over the bank, even though Trace's sister, Laila, was the member of the family who truly loved banking.

"Guilty," Lawrence admitted. "I assume you're here to say you'll back this loan of Megan's as long as she doesn't find out about it."

Mick nodded. "Draw up whatever paperwork you want. I'll sign it. Give her whatever she asked for."

Lawrence chuckled. "That's pretty much what I expected from you, Mick. Would it surprise you to know that I was going to recommend approval based solely on Megan's business plan?"

Mick didn't even try to hide his shock. "Really? The plan's solid?"

"You haven't seen it?"

"She wouldn't show it to me," he said, more disgruntled by that than ever. "Said she had to do this on her own."

"Good for her," Lawrence said approvingly. "I think you should let her." He gave Mick a knowing look. "And as a favor to you, I'll keep this little meeting just between us. Consider it a wedding present."

Feeling foolish, Mick nodded. "I appreciate that," he said. "I don't suppose you'd let me see that business plan, would you?"

"You probably should ask Megan for a glimpse of

it," Lawrence responded. "But considering our long history and knowing how this secrecy must be killing you, I'll let you see it." He handed it across the desk. "I need to run an errand. Those papers don't leave this room, understood?"

"Of course," Mick said, pulling out the annoying but necessary pair of reading glasses he kept tucked in his pocket these days.

Already absorbed, he barely noticed when Lawrence left the room. He'd only just made it through Megan's overview of the gallery's potential and taken his first glance at her financial estimates, when the door to Lawrence's office opened and Trace stepped in.

"I heard you were in here," his son-in-law said. He glanced at the papers in Mick's hand and added, "I assume that's Megan's business plan and her loan application."

Mick nodded guiltily. "Don't you dare say one word about this," he ordered Trace.

"That must mean you've gone behind Megan's back and are trying to interfere," Trace said knowingly.

"I'm looking out for her, that's all."

"Would she see it that way?"

Mick sighed. "Probably not, which is why this stays between the two of us."

"So, how much of a loan are you secretly guaranteeing?" Trace asked.

"None," Mick said. "Your father seems to think she doesn't need my backing."

At his disgruntled tone, Trace's grin spread. "That must have annoyed you."

"Why would it?" Mick lied. "I'm glad she can stand on her own two feet."

"Really?"

"Well, of course I am."

"Then you're more evolved than any of us suspected. Face it, Mick, you like having a finger in all these family pies. It makes you feel needed. How's it going to work now that you've seen that Megan doesn't need you?"

Though Trace was clearly teasing, Mick was taken aback by the question just the same. Maybe he had counted on Megan needing his financial backing to make this project of hers come together. On some level, he'd probably thought it would be one more thing binding them together.

He stood up abruptly. "I have to go."

Trace immediately looked guilty. "Hold on, Mick.

We both know Megan's coming back because she loves you. I never meant to suggest anything else."

"I know," Mick told him. "Don't worry about it. There's just someplace I need to be."

He had no idea where that place was, but he needed a quiet spot where he could think. When he and Megan were married before, he'd held the financial reins on the relationship, and still she'd left him. She'd loved him even then, but she'd moved away.

Now she was on this whole kick about being independent, doing her own thing on her own terms. Where did that leave him? For the first time since their reconciliation, Mick was genuinely uncertain about the future and a relationship that wasn't on terms he understood. He didn't like uncertainty. He didn't like it one damn bit!

He changed his mind about wanting to be alone. He needed to see Megan, get a few things straight. Megan had said something about stopping by Flowers on Main to see Bree, but when he got there, she'd already gone.

"Dad, is something wrong?" Bree asked worriedly, clearly trying to gauge his odd mood.

"I just need to see your mother, that's all."

"Why? Has something happened?"

He thought of the mess with Connor that was about to come to a head, the way Megan was striking out on her own. Not one blasted thing felt right. Just a few short weeks ago when she'd agreed to be his wife again, he'd been on top of the world. Now he had this feeling it was all slipping away.

He sat down and turned a bleak look on Bree. "Did you and your mother make any decisions about the flowers today?"

She frowned at the change of subject, but shook her head. "No, she said she wanted to think about it some more."

Mick's heart sank. It was just as he'd feared. She was already having second thoughts.

"She's going to cancel the wedding," he said eventually.

Bree looked at him with dismay. "Why on earth would you say that? She didn't even hint at such a thing to me. She's thrilled about marrying you again."

Mick wasn't buying it. "Just you wait and see."

"Is there something I don't know?" Bree asked, looking bewildered. "I swear to you everything seemed fine when she was here. She was a little nervous about her loan application, but that's all I noticed."

"Trust me, I know what I'm talking about," Mick said direly.

Bree gave him an impatient look. "If you actually believe what you're saying, then why are you here with me? Find Mom and fix whatever it is you think is broken."

"Did your mother say where she was going?"

"Back to the house, I think."

"Make me up one of those fancy bouquets of yours," he told her. "No roses. Tulips, maybe. Pink ones if you have them."

Bree looked at him as if he'd lost his mind. "Let me see what I have. I don't get a lot of requests for pink tulips two days before Thanksgiving."

"Which is why your mother will think they're special," he said. "What about lily of the valley? She loves that."

"I may have a few sprigs left from the wedding bouquet I made the other day. I'll see if they're still fresh."

Mick nodded. "Good. Now hurry up. I don't have a lot of time to waste."

He thought he'd done a pretty good job of courting Megan up to now, enough to get her to finally say yes to his proposal. Something told him, though, with all the hurdles left before them, he was going to have to kick the whole courting thing up a notch to actually get her down the aisle.

5

Even though the afternoon was cool and the wind brisk, Megan felt the need to go for a walk on the beach after she got home from seeing Lawrence and then Bree. She put on the fisherman's knit sweater Mick had brought her from Ireland one year, added a warm jacket and a scarf around her neck, then headed down to the beach.

She'd always been able to think more clearly with the breeze in her hair, the scent of salt in the air and the lap of waves against the shore. It should have been a good day. She'd been given the ideal location for her gallery, her meeting with Lawrence had gone smoothly enough, and it had been nice spending time with Bree making wedding and baby plans. Still, she felt vaguely uneasy, as if something was bound to go awry.

She'd walked along the sand for an hour, until the incoming tide warned her to turn back, when she spotted Mick coming toward her. He wasn't dressed nearly warmly enough, but he was so handsome he took her breath away. There was something about his windblown hair, the smile lines at the corners of his eyes and the way he looked in a pair of jeans that had the power to make her knees go weak even after all these years. The fact that he was carrying an armload of what looked incongruously like pink tulips made her smile.

"Did you walk halfway to Annapolis?" he inquired testily when he finally looked up and spotted her.

"Not quite," she said, then nodded toward the flowers. "Whose garden did you plunder? It can't have been anywhere around here this time of the year."

"I thought you might like something to remind you of spring," he said, holding them out awkwardly. "Bree tucked some lily of the valley in there, too."

Megan buried her face in the flowers, then beamed

at him. "I can smell it. Thank you. What's the occasion?"

He regarded her with an uneasy expression. "We've spent a lot of time lately worrying about other people and business, that kind of thing. I just wanted to put a little romance back into our relationship before we get off on the wrong track." He gave her an earnest look. "Meggie, whatever else happens, I don't want you to forget I love you."

Touched by the gesture and the heartfelt emotion in his words, she reached up and put her hand against his cheek. "As if I could ever forget that, Mick. I love you, too. I always have, even when I was most infuriated with you."

"Then promise me we won't let anything throw us off course," he said. "Whatever comes our way, we'll handle it together, talk it out."

His tone alerted her that he had something in particular on his mind. He wasn't the kind of man to encourage better communication just on a whim. She studied him with a narrowed gaze.

"What are you worried about, Mick? What is it you think might throw us off course?"

"Nothing specific," he insisted.

Megan kept her gaze locked with his and immediately saw his words for the lie they were. For all of his many flaws, he'd never been any good at shading the truth, much less lying outright. "Mick, tell me."

He took her free arm and tucked it though his, then pulled her closer to his side. "I'm just afraid that this disagreement with Connor will come between us, or that you'll get so caught up in your new business you won't have time for us."

"Now, wouldn't that be turning the tables?" she said lightly. "You'd have a taste of your own medicine." She regarded him seriously. "But I'm not marrying you so I'll have the chance to retaliate for the past. Surely you can't believe I would be that petty?"

Mick frowned at the comment. "Maybe that's not your intention, but things change, Megan. There'd be a certain irony, if they did."

"Do you honestly think that I, of all people, would let that happen, Mick? After all of my complaints when you put family on the back burner, how could you think for a second I would do the same thing?"

"You're awfully determined to make this new business of yours a success. Nobody understands that kind of drive better than I do."

She realized he was genuinely worried about such a thing coming to pass. "Mick, if it seems for even a minute that my priorities are out of order, you have my permission to call me on it. I want this business to succeed. I expect it to be fun and professionally satisfying, maybe even financially rewarding, but once you and I take our vows, whenever that is, you and our family will be my top priority."

"I would have said the same thing years ago," he reminded her, not sounding reassured. "I thought I was working so hard for my family, instead of stealing time from them."

"This won't be the same," she swore. "I promise. It's to be a small gallery, right here in Chesapeake Shores, not a nationally known architectural firm in demand from one coast to the other."

She studied him out of the corner of her eye. He didn't seem to be entirely satisfied by her response. "Mick, what else is going on in that head of yours?"

"I've just been thinking that here I am, semiretired, spending most of my time these days on volunteer projects, and you're about to launch a new venture. It takes time and commitment to do that successfully. How's it going to work if I say, let's pick up and go on a trip, on the spur of the moment? We're at a time in our lives when we should be able to be impulsive, to indulge ourselves. You're going to be all tied up with work."

"Ever heard of delegating?" she asked, then laughed. "Of course you haven't! That's why you were always racing around to every single job site around the country with barely a stop back here to take a breath."

"Need I remind you, I've changed?" he retorted indignantly. "Jaime's doing all the running now."

"Thank goodness for that," she said. "But, you see, I've always understood about delegating. I'm going to find an assistant manager who's as good at the job as I am, and then trust him or her to do it, just the way Phillip did with me."

He met her gaze. "Is that a promise?"

There was an urgency in his voice she didn't entirely understand, but she nodded. "Absolutely. Mick, we're going to make this work. If I didn't believe that, I never would have said yes to your proposal."

They walked in silence for a bit, still arm in arm, as the sun fell lower in the sky. The chill in the air turned more biting, and Megan shivered.

Mick glanced over at her and stopped. "I know just the thing to keep you warm," he said, a mischievous grin lighting his eyes.

"Hot chocolate?" she asked hopefully. "We're still fairly far from home. You don't have a thermos tucked in your pocket, do you? Or a flask with something stronger?"

"Better than that," he said, pulling her to him. He took the bouquet and set it on a boulder, then lowered his mouth to cover hers.

Heat spiraled through Megan, warming her down to her toes. It was the kind of heat that led straight to temptation. More than that, though, it was the kind of heat that reminded her that Mick O'Brien would always provide whatever she needed, from the most basic things in life to the most sweetly romantic and frivolous, like those poor, half-frozen tulips.

Whatever worries had gotten under his skin today to make him doubt the future, she didn't share them. At least not today. Right now she knew, above all else, that she was safe in this man's arms…and always would be.

On Wednesday morning, Mick found Nell in the kitchen muttering under her breath as she pulled the pumpkin pies for tomorrow's dinner from the oven. She'd be baking mincemeat next, then apple—that is, if she didn't let her temper get the better of her and walk out of the kitchen.

"Is there a problem, Ma?"

"You tell me," she said, glancing up at him with a scowl. "Connor just called to wish me a happy Thanksgiving. He says he's not coming home." She regarded him accusingly. "I thought you were going to fix this, Mick. Even through all the years you and your brothers have been sparring, there hasn't been a single holiday this family hasn't been together. Now's no time to change that."

Mick stilled, stricken by the reality that his argument with his son could well ruin the family holiday. He gave his mother a look filled with regret. "To be honest, I don't know how," he admitted.

"Of course you do," Nell said impatiently. "An apology would be a good start."

"I'm not the one—"

His mother cut him off. "Do you want to be right or do you want your son here for Thanksgiving?"

Mick winced.

"Megan will blame herself for this unless you tell her otherwise," Nell said. "Are you willing to let her shoulder the guilt when it should be you?"

"Guilt about what?" Megan asked, walking into

the kitchen just in time to overhear the end of the conversation.

Mick exchanged a look with his mother, but could think of no way to sugarcoat the news. "Connor won't be here tomorrow."

Predictably, Megan's face fell. "I see."

She turned and left the room, but not before Mick saw the sheen of tears in her eyes.

"See what I mean?" his mother said to him. "She's blaming herself."

"I'll go after her," Mick said, resigning himself to making some uncomfortable explanations.

"Let me," Nell said, handing him the pot holders. "Take the other pie out of the oven."

Since he had no earthly idea what he could possibly say to put a smile back on Megan's face, he let his mother go. But the minute he'd removed the pie from the oven and set it on the rack to cool, he grabbed his cell phone and called his son.

Connor answered, his voice wary. "What do you want, Dad?"

"I could lie and say I called to wish you a happy Thanksgiving, but we both know I'm not exactly pleased with you at the moment."

"That goes both ways," Connor said.

Mick tried to find the words to make amends without retracting his displeasure with Connor's stance. "Look, I know I told you to stay away, but I said it in the heat of the moment." He drew in a deep breath and forced himself to add, "Tomorrow's a holiday. You should be here celebrating with the rest of us."

"No, Dad, you were right to tell me not to come home," Connor said, surprising him. "I don't think I could sit there with everyone tomorrow and pretend I'm happy that you and Mom are back together. It's best that I stay away."

Mick had expected Connor to seize the opening, not throw it back in his face. Tamping down his frustration, he tried again. "Connor, I'm trying to say I'm sorry, that I made a mistake," Mick said. "Just accept my apology and come home."

"Too late. I've made other plans," Connor told him.

"What plans?"

"That doesn't matter," Connor said. "They don't include a visit to Chesapeake Shores and a meal I wouldn't be able to choke down."

Mick lost patience. "So instead you'll stay away and spoil the day for all of us? I didn't raise you to be that selfish, son."

"You didn't raise me at all," Connor retorted. "Gram did."

The barb was a direct hit, but Mick had an answer for it. "Well, we certainly know she didn't raise you to behave like this."

"How is this any different from the way you treat Uncle Thomas and Uncle Jeff?"

"Since both of your uncles and their families have always been welcomed here on holidays, no matter what my personal feelings, I'd say my actions speak for themselves."

"Well, I won't be a hypocrite."

"Boy, you need to watch who you're calling a hypocrite," Mick said grimly.

"Dad, I'm going to hang up before we both say things we're going to regret. I do wish you all a happy Thanksgiving. I've called Abby, Bree, Jess and Kevin."

"And what did they have to say when you announced you were boycotting the family celebration?"

"Pretty much what you said," he admitted. "That I'm being a selfish jerk."

"If you won't listen to me, maybe you should listen to them."

"I'm not coming, Dad. Sorry."

"I notice you didn't mention a call to your mother. I assume you have no intention of apologizing to her. You'll just let her feel guilty for keeping you away."

"Dad, you're the one who ordered me to stay away. You can do any explaining that's necessary."

He hung up before Mick could counter with another argument. Not that he had any. To his regret, Connor was proving he was more stubborn than all the rest of them combined, and that was saying something.

Late that night after Nell had gone to bed and the rest of the family had left, Megan turned to Mick.

"I've been thinking about this all day," she began quietly.

Mick knew what was coming and tried to forestall her. "Don't, Meggie."

"No, I have to say this, Mick. I think we need to postpone the wedding. I know I've mentioned the possibility before, but my mind's made up this time. How can we have a wedding when we've made Connor so miserable that he won't even celebrate Thanksgiving with the family? It would be wrong."

Mick winced. Whatever his mother had said to

Megan earlier, she'd left the truth to him. He drew in a deep breath, then admitted, "Connor's upset about the wedding, yes, but there's more. It isn't all about us."

She regarded him blankly. "More?"

"You know he and I had a disagreement," Mick began, feeling a flush climb into his cheeks. There was no way around an admission of his part in this now. Avoiding her gaze, he said, "What you don't know is that I told him to stay away."

Megan stared at him, clearly aghast. "You told your own son to stay away on Thanksgiving?"

"No, I told him to stay away, period."

"Oh, Mick, how could you? This is his home."

"Okay, I know it's bad. I was wrong, but I was angry," Mick said.

"That's no excuse."

"Look, I called him today and apologized, okay? I even pleaded with him to come tomorrow, but he turned me down flat." He gave her a defiant look. "That's the last time I grovel for anything with that boy."

"Somehow I doubt you did much groveling," Megan said wryly. "It's not in your nature. You probably just ordered him to come tomorrow the same way you'd told him to stay away."

"The point is, I made an effort. He refuses to do the same. He's just dug in his heels and is refusing to listen to reason."

Megan gave him a sad smile. "Does that sound like anyone else we know?"

"Me, I'm sorry to say." He touched a hand to her cheek. "Meggie, you know I'm right about not postponing the wedding because of this. We'll always be able to find an excuse for not moving forward, but all that really matters is whether we know in our hearts it's the right thing for us."

She shook her head. "It's not that simple, Mick. It was when we were barely out of our teens and first met, but now there are too many other people to consider."

"When Kevin was going through all of his heartache after Georgia died and you wanted to wait before telling anyone we were thinking of marrying again, I agreed," Mick reminded her. "This is different. Connor's just choosing to be impossible."

"No, he's still angry with me for leaving and with you for taking me back, to say nothing of how hurt he must have been when you banished him."

"That's his problem," Mick said stubbornly. "If he

won't even come home to spend a holiday with his family, how are we supposed to get through to him?"

"We need to give it more time," Megan insisted. "However long it takes."

Mick regarded her with a too-familiar unyielding look. "We're getting married New Year's Eve, Meggie, and that's that. I'll do whatever I can in the meantime to reach Connor, and you can do the same, but we are not postponing our wedding."

She frowned at the finality in his tone. This was the side of him that hadn't changed, one she wasn't sure she could tolerate even after all the other strides they'd made. Less than twenty-four hours ago, she'd been so certain of everything, so sure their relationship was solid. Now this.

She met his gaze. "Not even if I say it's important to me that all of our children are happy about this marriage, that going forward without their blessing is a deal-breaker?"

Mick hesitated, then shook his head. "Not even then."

She sighed. "Oh, Mick, then we've got bigger problems than Connor that we need to fix."

Though Nell, Abby, Bree and Jess had all come over Wednesday night to help with preparations for the big Thanksgiving feast, Mick couldn't enjoy having the women of his family all under one roof again. Megan's words still rang in his ears. He knew he'd pushed her too far, but how could he back down?

He heard laughter coming from the kitchen, but Megan hadn't joined in. He would have recognized her laugh at once. The joyful sound had always filled him with such a sense of peace and satisfaction.

Mick grabbed his jacket and a cigar and went out on the porch, even though the night air was about to hit the freezing mark.

He'd just settled into a rocker when the door opened and light spilled across the porch. He saw Megan hesitating in the doorway.

"Mick, it's too cold for you to be out here. Come back inside."

"I'm fine," he said gruffly.

"Well, Nell needs you. She wants you to get the turkey ready. It's too heavy for any of us to lift it into that big old tub of salt water and then carry it to the spare refrigerator in the mudroom so it can soak tonight. That's always been your job."

Even though it was the perfect excuse for joining the rest of the family, he wasn't anxious to risk a lecture from his outspoken daughters or another glimpse of the sadness in Megan's eyes.

"I'll be there in a couple of minutes," he told her.

Apparently his response didn't satisfy her, because she grabbed her jacket from the peg by the front door and came outside.

"Is this the way it's going to be tomorrow?" she asked.

"What do you mean?"

"You sitting off on the sidelines because you and I don't see eye to eye about Connor or the wedding," she said bluntly. "Because if it is, if this house is going to be filled with tension, I'll leave. I won't be responsible for everyone having a miserable holiday."

Alarm shot through him at the serious note in her voice. "No," he said at once. "You should be here for Thanksgiving. If you go now, we'll never put things to rights between us."

"Well, we're not doing that with you out here sulking, either."

"I wasn't sulking. I was smoking a cigar. I like a good cigar in the evening," he claimed.

"You also like being in the kitchen when it's crowded with family. This has always been one of your favorite holidays. Now come back inside.

Maybe you and I can just agree to disagree until Friday. Then we'll find some time to sit down on our own and talk things through."

"Seems reasonable," he said, taking heart. By Friday maybe Megan would see reason about not caving in to Connor's manipulative efforts to keep them apart.

"I'll just ask one thing of you in the meantime," she said. "We don't talk about the wedding in front of the others."

He stared at her incredulously. "Meggie, you know it's going to come up. Bree will want to discuss the flowers. I hear the twins have big plans for their role in the ceremony. They're dying to get your agreement. How can we put them off?"

"We'll just say the plans haven't been finalized. That's innocuous enough."

His gaze narrowed. "You won't say we've canceled?"

"No."

"Or postponed?"

"No, not until after we've talked on Friday and settled a few things."

He nodded. "That'll do."

"I'm only agreeing to that because I don't want the

holiday ruined and I don't want a lot of tension between us. Is that understood? My concerns are still
there. I won't claim our happiness at the cost of losing our son."

"Now you're being dramatic," he grumbled, not
able to hide his impatience. "Connor's not lost. He's
just stubborn."

"If we're not careful, it could come to that," Megan
insisted. Before he could respond, she held up her
hands in a gesture of surrender. "But from this moment on, the topic's off-limits until Friday."

Mick winced at the determination in her voice.
"Agreed," he said, because he had no choice. He was
no more eager to start a big family hullabaloo than
she was.

6

Thanksgiving day dawned with crisp fall air, bright blue skies and just a scattering of wispy white clouds floating overhead. Megan had a hundred blessings she knew she should be counting, but all she could think about were two overwhelming regrets. Her son wouldn't be here to share the holiday with the family, and Mick was being as impossible as ever.

Her talk with Nell the day before had been comforting, but had done nothing to dissuade her from her determination to postpone the wedding. Last night's conversation with Mick had only reinforced her stance. She just had to convince Mick she meant what she said and keep him from trying to bulldoze right over her very valid objections to moving forward with their wedding plans.

In the meantime, though, in the spirit of the holiday, she could at least make an overture to her son. It might not be welcome, but she had to try again to reach out to him. No matter how many tries it took, she would eventually get through to him. Anything less was unacceptable.

Carrying her cell phone onto the porch, she hit Connor's number on speed dial. The phone rang at least a dozen times, with no response and no answering machine pickup. She was about to give up when she finally heard his voice.

"Hello, Mother," he said, sounding annoyed and coolly distant.

"I wanted to wish you a happy Thanksgiving," she said cheerfully, determined to try to keep the conversation upbeat. "And to tell you how sorry I am that you won't be joining us."

He was silent for what seemed like an eternity before he responded with a grudging, "Happy Thanksgiving."

Ignoring his tone and continuing on the positive note she'd hoped to establish, she said, "You know, from the day each of you were born, you, your brother and your sisters have been right at the top of my list of blessings."

"And yet you walked away and left us behind," he responded bitterly. "I thought people were supposed to embrace blessings, not toss them aside like garbage."

"Oh, Connor, how many times do I have to tell you that it wasn't like that," she protested, unable to hide her dismayed reaction, yet knowing she would say the words over and over until he believed them. "I know just hearing me say how much I regret what happened doesn't mean anything, but it's true. There are so many things I would have done differently if I'd had the chance."

"In the end, though, you still would have left, wouldn't you?" he said accusingly.

She hesitated, but she knew a lie, even now, wouldn't serve her well. "Yes, I still would have left."

"Then that says it all," he said, his tone resigned.

"No," she corrected. "It only says how badly my marriage to your father had disintegrated at that time. It says nothing about how much I loved you."

"It doesn't matter now," he said dismissively.

"Obviously it does. Connor, please reconsider and come home today," she said hurriedly, sensing he was about to hang up. "It's not too late for all of us to be together. It's one day. Can't you do that much? We don't have to talk about our relationship or the wedding. Families should be together on Thanksgiving. We can deal with all the rest another time."

For the space of a heartbeat, she took hope from his silence. Unfortunately, it didn't last.

"No. I don't want to be where I'm not welcome," he said.

Though he sounded like a stubborn kid, Megan heard the hurt just below the surface. He'd always been like that, covering his deepest feelings so no one could detect his vulnerabilities. For many years he'd covered with wit and laughter. Now he relied on belligerence.

"Connor, before I let you go, I want to make one thing absolutely clear," she said, hoping she could get through to him. "No matter how angry your father was, no matter what he said, he loves you with his whole heart. So do I. And as long as either of us is around, this will be your home and you will be welcome here."

She could tell he was taking in her words, probably deciding whether he could trust them. She kept talking.

"Families fight," she said. "People say things in the heat of the moment. You must know that, given the number of arguments you and Kevin had growing up. But when push comes to shove, O'Briens stick together. We're bound together by love. I know what it was like to be outside that circle. I was outside, because I chose to be, just as you're choosing to stay away now. When the time comes and you're ready, you *will* be welcomed back, just as I have been. I promise you that. Just, please, don't stay away too long, because as time goes by, it gets harder and harder to go back."

She waited, desperately wanting her words to sink in, praying for a response.

Instead, all he said was goodbye.

"I love you, Connor," she said, hoping he'd stayed on the line long enough to hear her, hoping he believed she meant it.

She closed her cell phone, tucked it in her pocket, then let her tears fall.

By the time Megan gathered her composure, a few early-bird family members had started to arrive. Nell had once again taken charge in the kitchen, ordering everyone around with the efficiency and determination of a drill sergeant.

The kitchen table groaned under the weight of pies, bowls of homemade cranberry relish, trays of rolls ready for the oven, casseroles filled with sweet potatoes topped with marshmallows or green beans. Megan breathed in the once-familiar scents with satisfaction.

"I've missed this," she told Nell. "Nothing smells like your kitchen on Thanksgiving morning."

"You don't object to me taking over?" Nell asked. "This should be your domain now."

"It will always be yours," Megan contradicted. "Even if you decide to move back to your own cottage, when it comes to family occasions, I will always gladly defer to you. I never did have the knack of organizing meals for a family this size, especially on holidays. I could barely get supper on the table when it was just the kids and me."

Nell gave her a disbelieving look. "Don't be downplaying your cooking skills just to placate me. You're a fine cook."

"Maybe of a few basics," Megan conceded. "But you're the one with the real flair for entertaining so many people and making it look easy. Now, tell me what I can do to help."

"The twins set the table last night. I didn't want to insult them by hovering, but I took a look after they went home," Nell said with an amused shake of her head. "It could use a finishing touch. Would you mind?"

"Absolutely not," Megan said, grateful to have a task that would give her some time on her own. Her emotions were still raw after her conversation with Connor. The longer she had to pull herself together before facing Mick or her far-too-intuitive daughters, the better. One thing that conversation had done was to add more reinforcement to her determination to postpone the wedding.

She was in the dining room straightening place settings and folding the napkins more neatly, when Carrie and Caitlyn bounded in with their usual exuberance. Nine now, the twins still wore matching outfits much of the time, but their personalities were so unique, it made telling them apart easy enough. She smiled at the sight of them in their fancy dresses with lace at the collar and their shiny Mary Jane shoes. They were dressed like perfect little ladies, but their expressions were pure imp.

"Don't you look beautiful," she said. "Happy Thanksgiving."

"Happy Thanksgiving," Caitlyn replied dutifully, though she looked as if she were bursting at the seams to talk about something else. She was bouncing on her tiptoes and looking at her sister, who regarded Megan solemnly.

"Grandma Megan, me and Caitlyn need to talk to you about something really, really important," Carrie said.

"Okay," Megan replied, hunkering down in front of them. "Tell me."

"Can Caitlyn and me be in the wedding?" Carrie asked in a rush, her eyes bright with excitement. "We've been flower girls before, but we think we're too big for that now. We should probably be bridesmaids."

"And we want to wear red velvet dresses," Caitlyn chimed in. "Mommy says it'll clash with our red hair, but we don't care. Red's our very favorite color. And it's a Christmas color, so it's perfect." She regarded Megan hopefully. "Don't you think so?"

Abby walked in just in time to overhear. "Girls, didn't I tell you that you should wait to see what your grandmother wants for her wedding? It's her big day and she probably has her own ideas."

"But she needs to know how really, really important this is to us," Carrie argued. "Otherwise, how can she decide what kind of wedding to have?"

Mick had warned Megan about this, but she hadn't been prepared for how awful it would feel to disappoint Carrie and Caitlyn when their hearts were set on this holiday-season wedding. She gave Abby a helpless look, then faced her granddaughters.

"As soon as I start focusing on my wedding plans, I promise I'll think about your offer, girls," she assured them.

"But aren't you planning now?" Caitlyn asked, looking puzzled. "It's only a little while till New Year's Eve. I looked at one of Mom's bridal magazines. There's a lot to do for a wedding. I could help you make a list."

"There is a lot to do," Megan agreed. "And I will certainly appreciate your help when the time comes. Now why don't you track down your Grandpa Mick? I think he bought a new game for you to play while we're getting dinner ready."

"Grandpa Mick's watching football," Caitlyn said, sounding despondent. "So are Trace and Uncle Jake

and Uncle Kevin. We can't find Uncle Connor anywhere. He's the one who usually plays with us."

Abby directed an apologetic look toward Megan,
then frowned at her daughters. "I told you Uncle
Connor might not be here," she said. "Now scoot."

"But it's Thanksgiving," Carrie protested. "Everybody comes for Thanksgiving!"

Abby scowled. "Go find your grandfather and
Trace. Tell them they have to set up a game for all
you kids to play. Tell them your mother said so."

After the girls had scampered off, Megan sank
down on a chair. Abby sat next to her.

"I'm sorry, Mom. They don't realize that Connor's
being a gigantic pain."

"He's entitled to his feelings," Megan said. "You
all are."

"But the rest of us have seen that there are two
sides to the story. You've worked really hard to reconnect with us."

"And apparently I haven't worked hard enough
to reconnect with Connor." She glanced at Abby. "I
called him this morning. I asked one more time that
he reconsider and come home today. He turned me
down."

"Of course he did. He never could back down

once he's taken a stance," Abby said. "After we get through today, I intend to track him down myself and tell him what I think of his behavior."

Megan gave her a wry look. "Do you honestly think that will help?"

"Probably not," Abby conceded. "But I'll feel better."

"It's not about you feeling better," Megan reminded her oldest daughter. "It's about getting Connor on board with your father and me reconciling." She lifted her chin. "Which is why I've told your father we need to postpone the wedding."

Abby looked stricken. "Mom, no!"

"I'm not bending on this. It's the right thing to do," Megan insisted. "Maybe it's even for the best. I was so sure your father had changed, but the past few days, I don't know, he still likes to do everything on his own terms."

"Meaning?"

"For starters, he went ahead and leased a place on Shore Road for the art gallery without even consulting me. He said it was a wedding present."

"Okay," Abby said slowly, clearly not understanding the problem. "Is there something wrong with the space?"

"No, it's perfect, but it's way too expensive. I certainly couldn't have afforded to lease it on my own."

Abby continued to look confused. "It sounds as if he wanted to do something nice for you."

"He did," Megan said. "I can see that, but I also see that he's going about things in his usual style, as if what I think doesn't matter."

"I suppose I can see your point, but that's just one thing, Mom. Maybe you're being too hard on him. You know he's changed. We've all seen that. Leasing a store space for you sounds really thoughtful."

Megan regarded her quizzically. "Abby, you know how your father is. Do you honestly think I'm making too much of him making decisions like this without even speaking to me?"

"To be perfectly honest, I do. Didn't you leave him years ago because he was being thoughtless and neglectful? Now he's stepping up to be the kind of man you always said you wanted, and you're criticizing him for that, too."

Megan winced. "In other words, I'm being ungrateful and sending contradictory messages."

"Seems that way to me. As for postponing the wedding because of Connor, don't let him have that power over you," Abby pleaded. "If he sees weakness, he'll use it to get his way. That's why he's such a good lawyer. He knows exactly how to exploit his opponent's weaknesses."

"It just makes me so sad knowing that I've chased him away on a day like today and that he won't be here for the wedding because he objects to it so strenuously."

"Forget today. Dad's more responsible for Connor not being here than you are. As for the wedding, there's still plenty of time before New Year's Eve. I imagine the rest of us can be pretty persuasive if we put our minds to it. Connor will be here."

Megan gave her a wry look. "I'm not sure I want him coming just because you all have ganged up on him and bullied him into it."

Abby grinned. "What if we make him think it's his idea?"

Megan shook her head. "Christmas is a time of miracles, but I doubt if you can pull that off even then."

Amazingly, with the house filled with so many people, virtually no one mentioned Connor or his absence. Even when Jeff arrived with his family and Thomas showed up moments later, Connor's name never crossed anyone's lips. Megan suspected they'd been warned to avoid the subject. It was a rare display of sensitivity from a family known for blurting out whatever was on their minds.

Though she was grateful not to have Connor's actions dissected, Megan felt guilty knowing that they were censoring themselves because of her. Worse, she couldn't get past the image of Connor somewhere all alone on a holiday. Hopefully he was at least sharing the day with friends. She hadn't even given up on the hope that he'd have a change of heart and join them.

She went back onto the porch, staring out into the gathering darkness, hoping to see headlights coming up the coastal highway. She was battling disappointment when someone scooped her up from behind and twirled her around.

"Megan O'Brien, I never thought I'd live to see you back in this house again," Thomas said, beaming as he set her back on her feet. "Are you sure you want to go another round with that obstinate brother of mine when I'm available?"

Megan laughed at his teasing. Thomas's lighthearted banter had always raised her spirits, and she'd known never to take his flirtatious remarks to heart. Mick was capable of blarney, but Thomas had raised it to an art form.

"If there's one thing I know about you," she told him now, "it's that you're every bit the workaholic your brother used to be. Why would I let myself in for that again?"

"And you think Mick has reformed?" Thomas asked skeptically.

"I know he has," she said with confidence.

Mick emerged from the house in time to overhear. He scowled at his younger brother with mock indignation. "Are you out here trying to steal my woman?" he demanded. "Why would she want you? You're hardly a prize."

"But I am handsome and charming and will treat her like a queen," Thomas claimed, giving Megan a wink.

Mick put a possessive arm around her waist. "Go find your own woman, if you can. Those two wives of yours didn't leave you for no reason. Obviously you have a few serious flaws that exceed even mine."

Thomas didn't look offended by the jab. For one thing, they all knew Mick's remark was true. For another, Thomas was used to Mick taking any opportunity to take a genial poke at him.

"Pot calling the kettle black," Thomas retorted. "Megan had plenty of reasons to walk out on you, as well."

Listening to them, she shook her head. "It's lovely to see that you two still squabble like little boys," she told them. "Shouldn't one of you be more mature by now?"

"I hope I never get so old that I can't take on the likes of him," Mick said.

"Age and maturity are two different matters," Thomas commented. "I'm not surprised you didn't know that, big brother."

Megan laughed. "If Nell overhears the two of you, you'll wind up eating Thanksgiving dinner all alone in the kitchen. She won't tolerate fussing at her table." She studied the two men. "I thought you reached some kind of truce when you were both conspiring to get Kevin and Shanna together."

"Now that was a worthy cause," Thomas said. "Kevin comes to work happy every day now. He's not the sad, broken man he was after Georgia died."

"Amen to that," Mick said in a rare display of consensus.

"There now," Megan said happily. "See how easy it is to get along? Let's go inside for dinner right this second, before this jovial mood wears off. See if you can't carry it over to include Jeff, as well."

"Now you're just dreaming," Mick said, but he gave her a smile that belied his words. He'd keep the peace today, because it was what Nell expected and what the occasion deserved.

As they walked into the jam-packed dining room, they found chaos. Even though there was plenty of room at the table for everyone, the kids especially were jockeying for position as if they feared being left out. The parents were making a mostly futile effort to bring order. It was Nell who tapped on a crystal goblet until she finally had every one's attention.

"Did you not see the place cards I put on this table just to avoid this kind of scene?" she inquired. "Now find your places quietly, or you'll eat in the kitchen." She gave all of them a stern look. "And I'm not just warning the children, either."

To Megan's amusement, order reigned immediately. Nell might be diminutive, but her words carried weight with this family. Megan noted that even though Nell expected her sons to get along, she'd been careful to keep them well separated. It was easy enough to do, given the size of the crowd.

They had all barely settled down and Mick was

about to say grace, when the doorbell rang. Megan's spirits immediately rose, even though the likelihood of Connor ringing the doorbell, rather than walking in, was slight.

"I'll get it," she said, then hurried into the foyer.

She opened the front door still half expecting to find Connor, but instead she found a pretty young woman with blond hair, sad eyes and an infant in her arms. Wrapped in a blue blanket and wearing a warm blue jacket, the baby looked to be at least six months old, possibly older, and, to Megan's shock, there was no mistaking the coal-black hair and striking blue eyes of the child as anything other than an O'Brien's.

She opened the door wider and stepped aside, determined to be gracious despite her shock and confusion. "Come in. Please. It's far too chilly for the baby to be outside."

The young woman shook her head. "I can't stay," she said, then held the bundled-up baby out toward Megan.

Instinctively, Megan took the boy into her arms, cradling him against her chest. He squirmed in protest, but quieted as she rubbed his back.

"I don't understand," she said, her gaze on the woman's face. "Why are you here?"

"Because of the baby. He needs his father," she said, already taking a step back.

It was every bit as bad as Megan had feared. "Don't you want to come in and talk about this?"

"No." She cast a look of longing at the baby. "His name's Mick," she said, leaving Megan's breath lodged in her throat. "Michael Devlin O'Brien, actually."

His name was Mick? How could that possibly be? Megan's thoughts reeled.

The solemn little boy in Megan's arms stirred at the mention of his name and reached for his mother, but she was already at the bottom of the steps.

She swallowed hard, and her eyes shimmered with tears. "Tell his father I love him, but I can't do this alone."

Megan gasped, even though she'd been anticipating something like that from the moment she'd laid eyes on the child.

The woman gave her a pleading look. "Please take care of my son. Someday tell him that his mom loved him enough to let him go."

Before Megan could utter a single word, the woman turned and ran off into the night. A moment later, still standing there in shock, Megan heard a car start, then saw headlights wind down the long driveway to the coastal road.

She stared down at the now-whimpering child, her heart aching for too many reasons to count. Worst of all, it seemed she didn't know her soon-to-be-husband, ex-husband, whatever, half as well as she'd thought she did.

7

Mick took one look at Megan's ashen face and the infant in her arms and bolted from his chair. He went to her side, but she turned away from him. It was clear she was furious with him for some reason. Mick couldn't make any sense of it, not her attitude and definitely not the sudden appearance of this baby.

"What the devil?" he demanded, even as the child started crying in earnest.

Though she was clearly as perplexed as he was, Abby stood and calmly took the boy from her mother, then scowled at Mick. "Lower your voice, Dad. You're scaring him."

Apparently sensing that things were about to get wildly out of hand, Jess quickly came around the table to Abby's side. Like the rest of them, she seemed unable to tear her gaze away from the baby who seemed so obviously to be an O'Brien.

"Why don't I take him?" Jess offered. "There's bound to be something I can mash up for him to eat, while you all sort this out. Do we have any baby bottles, Gram?"

"I think there are two or three left from when Davy was a baby," Nell said distractedly, her gaze riveted on the child in Jess's arms. "They should be in the back of the pantry. They might be packed up in a box, though."

"Not to worry. I'll find them," Jess said.

"Take the rest of the kids with you," Abby suggested. "They don't need to hear any of this." Carrie and Caitlyn, especially, were staring at the newcomer with wide-eyed curiosity.

"Whose baby is that?" Carrie asked.

That was certainly the uppermost question on everyone's mind, Mick thought.

"We don't know," Abby told her daughter and hurried her along to the kitchen.

"Is it a boy? Why is he here?" Carrie wanted to know, determinedly hanging back.

Out of the mouths of babes, more good questions, Mick noted. Though he was aware of all the undercurrents in the room, he couldn't seem to tear his gaze away from Megan, who was looking everywhere except at him. Judging from her tight-lipped expression she was still seething and trying very hard not to show it in front of everyone. He had the distinct impression she was torn between bolting and exploding.

"Okay, now that the children have left the room, let's look at this situation calmly," he said mildly. He took his seat again, as did Abby and then with obvious reluctance, Megan.

"Megan, what's going on here? Where did that baby come from?" Mick asked, echoing Carrie.

Megan finally looked in his direction with an expression that cut right through him.

"That's what I'd like to know," she said, her voice like ice. "A young woman just dropped him off and said he belonged with his father."

An audible gasp greeted her announcement. It was

the first time in forever that this family had been in unison on anything, Mick thought irritably.

He regarded Megan with confusion. "His father? What the hell is she talking about?"

"All I know is what she said," she insisted, her gaze locked with his. "Did I forget to mention that his name is Mick? Michael Devlin O'Brien, in fact."

"Holy mother of God," Nell murmured, sketching a cross over her chest. Thomas quickly moved to Nell's side and put an arm around her, all the while staring at Mick incredulously.

Mick could practically feel his blood pressure skyrocket at the unfairness of the implied accusation. He scowled at his mother and his brother. "Save your prayers, Ma. This is not my son, and anyone who says otherwise is lying!"

"Then how do you explain him being dropped off here?" Megan asked. "I've seen enough O'Brien babies over the years to know he bears a striking family resemblance. Plus the name would seem to be more than a coincidence."

Mick was at a loss to explain any of it, but then Kevin spoke, his voice shaky.

"I may know," he said.

"Then you need to explain fast," Mick told him. "What do you know about this? Is the boy yours?"

At Mick's blunt question, Shanna turned on her husband with a dismayed expression. "Is he?" she murmured, sounding stunned.

"Of course not," Kevin said impatiently. "I can't be a hundred percent certain, because I've never seen the baby before, but I'm pretty sure Connor must be the father."

"Connor!" Mick bellowed. "You can't be serious."

"I can't swear to it," Kevin stressed. "It just fits with a few things I do know for a fact."

Mick couldn't accept what had to be outrageous speculation on his older son's part. "You must be wrong," Mick argued flatly. "Connor couldn't possibly have kept this kind of secret from the rest of us."

"Of course he could," Bree said, speaking up for the first time. "Connor's as tight-lipped as anyone I've ever known. That's why his clients trust him."

"I agree," Kevin said, giving Mick a challenging look. "Have any of us ever been invited to his apartment in Baltimore? No. When he wants to see us, he comes here. He never talks about who he's involved with or even if he's involved with anyone.

Dad, you and I were talking about that very thing just the other day."

Mick thought back to that conversation. He still couldn't grasp the magnitude of the deception Connor might have perpetrated on all of them.

"So you're saying your brother has been hiding not only a woman but a baby from us?" Mick said. "Why the hell would he do that? We're family." He tried to think of an explanation that made sense. "Is there something wrong with this woman? Does he think we wouldn't approve? Why else would he never once bring her here? Did the two of them sneak off and get married?" Mick had at least a hundred questions. Unfortunately the only man who could answer most of them wasn't here.

Feeling completely out of sorts over this turn of events, he scowled at the one son who was here. "Kevin, what exactly do you know about all this?"

"I've already told you most of what I know," Kevin insisted. "I saw a woman at his apartment when I stopped by unexpectedly months ago. She was obviously pregnant. Connor looked as embarrassed as hell that I'd caught her there, but he didn't offer any explanation. He barely even introduced us."

"What did he say?" Mick asked. "Did he say she

was a friend? His wife? Some woman he was helping out?"

"Believe me, he barely mentioned a name, and it
wasn't O'Brien. I don't think they're married, but I
do think she was living there. There were some cozy
touches in the apartment, things only a woman would
do, like a quilt hanging on the wall, some fresh flowers in vases, that kind of thing."

"And you never thought to say a word to the rest
of us?" Mick said incredulously, just as Bree muttered, "Speaking of tight-lipped."

Kevin frowned at both of them. "It wasn't any of
my business. Whatever was going on, it was Connor's news to share. I just chatted for a minute and
got out of there. It was damned awkward, to be honest."

Mick studied the rest of his family. Everyone appeared as shocked as he was feeling. Megan still
looked as if she were reeling. Hard as he tried, he
couldn't think of a thing to say that might make her
feel better. The more he thought about it, the more
frustrated he became. He slammed a hand down on
the table so hard the china rattled.

"None of this makes a bit of sense," he declared.
"What kind of person lives with someone, has a child

with her and never says a single word about it to his family? It's just not possible." He scowled at Jeff's sons. Matthew was twenty-four, Luke twenty-two, both of them plenty old enough to have created this situation. "What about you two? Do you know anything about this?"

Jeff bristled at Mick's hint that they could be involved. "Don't start throwing accusations at my sons," Jeff said heatedly. "If you can't control Connor, that's your problem. That child in there doesn't belong to Matthew or Luke." Despite his adamant claim, he cast a frown in their direction, then looked relieved when they nodded.

"We don't know yet that Connor had anything to do with this, either," Mick insisted. "For all we know some woman got pregnant, maybe knew Connor in passing or something about this family and decided to leave a baby on our doorstep because she knew we're rich enough to care for it. Mark my words, she'll be back to make even more outrageous claims in a few days."

This time it was Megan who spoke. "I don't think so. She sounded totally sincere. She wanted her baby to be with his father."

Mick refused to accept that. "I'll say it again.

There's no reason Connor would keep something like this a secret."

"Of course there is," Kevin countered. "You know how adamantly Connor's opposed to marriage, because of…" His voice trailed off as he glanced apologetically at Megan. "Well, you know why. At the same time, he knew if any of us knew about the baby, we'd be all over him to get married."

"Well, of course we would," Mick declared furiously. "O'Briens step up to the plate in this kind of situation, I don't care what kind of so-called issues they have."

No one seemed to have any response to that.

Eventually his brother Thomas stood up. "Mick, I think Jeff and I and the rest of us need to clear out and let you all deal with this crisis."

"You're family, too," Nell protested. Though she looked shaken by the news, she clearly wanted to salvage whatever was left of the holiday celebration. "And we haven't even had our meal yet. Shouldn't we at least try to share our Thanksgiving meal before everyone leaves?"

"We'll take some turkey and a pie home, if that's okay," Jeff's wife, Jo, said. "It's fine, Nell. Thomas is right. You don't need the rest of us chiming in with our opinions. The situation is complicated enough."

Mick appreciated the gesture. Jo had always been a sensible woman. "Thank you. I apologize for this, and Jeff, I'm sorry for trying to drag Matthew and Luke into it."

To his surprise, Jeff paused by his chair and gave his shoulder a reassuring squeeze. "No need to apologize, Mick. And before you go off the deep end with Connor, make sure you get all the facts, okay? If there's one thing I've learned over the years with Matt, Luke and Susie, it's that things aren't always what they seem."

Mick glanced toward the kitchen, where the baby could be heard whimpering. "I'd say these facts speak for themselves."

"Not necessarily," Jeff insisted. "Give the boy a chance to explain."

It was Nell who walked his brothers and Jeff's family through the kitchen to wrap up some meals to go. His own family sat where they were in stunned silence until they heard the kitchen door close. Then everyone began talking at once. Mick held up a hand and demanded silence. He turned back to Kevin.

"Are you absolutely sure you don't know anything else?"

"Not much," Kevin said. "The next time I saw Connor, I asked him about the woman I'd met, but mostly he just blew me off. He did tell me that her name is Heather and they've been together since college."

Megan's eyes widened as Kevin spoke. "Of course. I should have seen it right away," she murmured.

Mick's head was spinning. "Seen what?"

"Just now, at the front door, I thought she looked vaguely familiar," Megan said. "I saw them together years ago at one of Connor's college baseball games. She was a cheerleader."

"I think she was," Kevin said, regarding her with surprise.

"You were at Connor's games?" Mick asked.

She frowned at him. "That's hardly the point." She whirled on Kevin. "Call your brother," she said decisively. "Tell him to get over here now. If he balks, you might mention that his son is here and that pretty much trumps whatever he's feeling about me, his father or the wedding."

"I'll call him myself," Mick said, but Megan put a hand on his arm.

"It'll go better coming from his brother. Besides,

I owe you an apology for thinking even for a second that you could be responsible for this."

"Understandable," Mick said, conceding how things must have looked at first glance.

Megan sighed. "But it's yet another reason why we shouldn't be rushing into marriage again."

He stared at her incredulously, unable to fathom how she'd made such a leap. "Why on earth would you say that? One thing has nothing to do with the other."

"Oh, Mick, don't you see?" she whispered. "If I could doubt you, even for an instant, then clearly I haven't worked out all the issues between us."

All Mick could see was that this latest roadblock wasn't even of his own doing. He felt like hitting something or someone—Connor came to mind—but knew it would be counterproductive. Instead he needed to focus on cleaning up this mess his son had made and winning Megan's trust in time to take that walk down the aisle on New Year's Eve. It was getting more and more difficult to have faith he could pull that off.

After Kevin left to try to reach Connor, everyone remaining at the table pretty much agreed that dinner was over. No one had any appetite for the food, which had gone cold by now anyway.

"We'll have leftovers later, when everything's calmed down," Nell said, taking charge. "I'll package a few things up for all of you. Bree, you look exhausted. Jake, why don't you take her home? Abby, you and Trace should probably take the twins home. I'll send the food over later." She turned to Shanna. "Do you want to take Davy and Henry home now? We'll see that Kevin gets home as soon as things calm down a bit."

Shanna nodded. "I think that's a good idea. Don't you want help with cleaning up, though?"

"Jess and I can take care of that," Megan assured her. Right now Jess was upstairs trying to get the baby settled into Davy's old crib, which Mick had brought down from the attic.

"Then I'll get the boys," Shanna said. "I'll speak to Kevin on my way out and let him know someone will give him a ride."

"I'm so sorry about all of this," Megan said, giving her a hug. "This family's always been full of surprises, but today may have set a whole new standard."

Abby gave Megan a fierce hug. "I'll talk to you

later, okay? Try not to let this upset you too much, and keep Dad from blowing a fuse once Connor turns up. If you need backup, Trace and I are only a phone call away."

"Thanks, sweetie."

When everyone had taken off, Megan gave Nell a weary look. "Do you honestly think we're going to be able to sort this out?"

Nell nodded. "Of course."

"How?"

"I have no idea, but Jeff is right. We have to give Connor a chance to explain." She touched Megan's cheek. "Whatever you do, though, don't let this be one more thing to come between you and Mick."

Megan sighed. "How can I not? You saw what happened earlier. I practically accused him of fathering a child with a woman young enough to be his daughter."

"Mick knows why you leaped to such an outrageous conclusion," Nell said. "I might have done the same thing. In fact, for a moment there, I did. Mick saw it in my face, I'm sure. You heard the way he snapped at me, and rightfully so."

"It was only for a moment, though," Megan said. "You've always had more faith in Mick than I have."

"That suggests that I'm unaware of his flaws," Nell chided. "We both know that's not true. I understood why you needed to leave him years ago, even if I didn't like how things worked out with you leaving the children behind."

Megan sighed. "I made such a mess of things," she admitted. "I think I've earned forgiveness for some of my mistakes, whether I deserve it or not, but with Connor things just seem to get more and more complicated."

Nell regarded her with surprise. "Surely you're not blaming this latest twist on anything you did?"

"I set a very poor example for him when it comes to demonstrating that marriage is supposed to be forever and that adults should fight to work things out, especially when there are children involved. It's little wonder he feels the way he does about marriage. Nor is it surprising that he's not taking responsibility for his own son."

"I think we can blame his career for some of that," Nell said dryly. "He spends most of his time with couples who are bitterly fighting over possessions and money. You and Mick never did that."

"No. I just walked off and left my children behind. You tell me which is worse," Megan said bleakly.

"That's all water under the bridge," Nell declared. "Connor's a grown man. He's been making his own decisions for some time now. Apparently, he hasn't been making very good ones."

Megan thought of Heather and the sorrow she'd seen in her eyes. "I feel so bad for that young woman. She looked absolutely brokenhearted. She looked the way I felt the day I left Mick. I tried to stop her. I asked her to stay, but her mind was obviously made up. If Kevin is right and she and Connor have been living together for some time, I wonder what on earth happened to make her do something this desperate."

"We've no way of knowing," Nell said pragmatically. "We'll just have to wait and see."

The kitchen door opened and Mick walked in. He poured himself a drink, then sat down at the table. "Kevin hasn't reached Connor. Jess finally managed to get the baby to sleep. She'll be down in a minute."

Nell suddenly looked every one of her eighty-some years. "If you don't mind, then, I think I'll go upstairs to my room and rest for a bit. Suddenly I'm feeling very tired."

Megan regarded her with alarm. She'd never heard Nell admit to being exhausted before. "Are you okay?"

"Just a bit too much excitement, I'm sure," Nell said. She nodded toward Mick. "Besides, I think the two of you have things to discuss without me underfoot."

Megan waited until Nell had gone before facing Mick. "Once again, I owe you an apology for what I thought earlier."

Mick waved it off. "Let it go. I have." He gave her an astonishingly vulnerable look. "What are we going to do about this mess? That baby's apparently our grandchild, Megan, and we didn't even know of his existence."

"We're not going to do anything, except to take care of that little boy until Connor turns up here," she said emphatically. "This is his situation to resolve."

"Maybe so, but it's landed on my doorstep," Mick argued. "I'd say that gives me a right to speak my mind."

Megan regarded him ruefully. "If you had any of the facts, it might. Until you do, keep an open mind, Mick. I mean it. Connor needs our support and guidance now, not a lot of shouting."

"I don't—"

Megan gave him an incredulous look that cut off his words.

"Okay, I'll keep a hold on my temper," he promised.

They sat in silence for several minutes, Mick sipping his drink and Megan her tea. When Mick finally looked up and met her gaze, there was an expression of awe in his eyes. Megan had seen it before when each of their children had been born.

"Did you take a good look at him?" he asked. "He's an O'Brien, that's for sure. Strong, too. He got a grip on my finger and wouldn't let go."

Megan smiled at the note of pride in his voice. "That's the thing about O'Briens," she said. "Once they get a hold on you, none of them will let go."

Even with years and miles between them, Mick still held her heart as securely today as he had on the day they'd wed. If only she could be sure that would be enough to get them through whatever lay ahead.

Mick awoke after midnight, aware that Megan had left his bed. He knew, though, even before he heard the baby's giggles, where he'd find her.

Pulling on a robe, he walked down the hall to Connor's old room where they'd set up the portable crib and a few other things to turn the room into a makeshift nursery. The only light came from a night-light and from the moon spilling through the window.

Megan sat in the same rocker in which she'd rocked all of their children to sleep, holding the baby in her arms and tickling him. He giggled some more and tried to grab onto the necklace she was wearing.

"Oh no, you don't, my little angel," she murmured, taking the diamond pendant from his little hand and putting it behind her neck, where it wouldn't tempt him. "Your Grandpa Mick gave me that necklace years and years ago. I'm not letting you break it."

"I'd buy you another," Mick said, taking in the picture the two of them made, bathed in moonlight. He'd never seen anything lovelier.

"Did I wake you?" Megan asked, lifting her gaze to his. "I'm sorry."

"I always know when you're not in my bed," he said. "I didn't have a decent night's sleep all the years you were gone."

She gave him a disbelieving look. "There's that blarney again, little one. Your grandpa is full of it."

"I'm only speaking the truth," Mick insisted, then tucked a finger under the baby's chin and gazed into those solemn blue eyes that were so like Connor's. "But I am here to tell you that a bit of blarney can serve you well. It's gotten me out of many a tough jam, some of them with this very woman."

A toothless grin spread across the baby's face, as if he understood exactly what Mick was suggesting.

"Do not be giving him ideas," Megan ordered, though there was a hint of laughter in her eyes. "I suppose I should put him down and let him go back to sleep, but I can't bring myself to let him go. I've missed holding a baby in my arms. I had far too few chances to do it with Carrie and Caitlyn, and I completely missed being around Davy when he was this age."

"Something tells me you're going to have plenty of time with this one," Mick said, then sighed sorrowfully. "What is wrong with our son that he's ignored all of Kevin's calls?"

"He could have gone out of town for the holiday," Megan suggested.

"Without his cell phone?" Mick asked. "I sometimes think that phone has been surgically attached to his ear. Ever since he joined that highfalutin law firm, it's like he's scared to death to miss a call. No, he's ignoring this because he doesn't want to face any of us."

"Can you blame him?" Megan asked. "He has to know what's going to happen the second he shows his face."

"He should have thought of that months ago," Mick said, then recalculated. "No, more like a year and a half ago or more, when he got that girl pregnant in the first place."

"He's not the first young man who didn't think things through when he got involved with a woman," Megan reminded him.

"He's the first O'Brien who didn't," Mick retorted.

Megan gave him a disbelieving look. "Is that so? You and I took our share of chances before we got married."

"But we knew marriage was in our future. There was never any question about that. If Connor's so dead set on staying single, then he has no business putting a woman at risk of getting pregnant."

"You're suggesting he steer clear of women?" Megan said, looking amused. "Connor took an interest in girls before he turned twelve. I think celibacy is a pretty unrealistic expectation."

"Hasn't the boy ever heard of protection?" Mick grumbled. "I seem to remember giving him several lectures on that very topic."

"And I'm sure he heard every word," Megan consoled him. "Things happen, Mick. That's just the way life is. The point is, we have to deal with the here and now."

"Fine by me," Mick said. "Do you see Connor anywhere around dealing with it?"

"He'll be here," Megan said with confidence. "And then we'll figure this out."

She put the now-sleeping baby back into the crib, then took Mick's hand. "Let's try to get some sleep before he wakes up again. Something tells me tomorrow's going to be just as chaotic as today turned out to be. We'll want to be rested."

Mick allowed her to lead him back to bed, then pulled her into his arms. But even as Megan fell asleep, he lay there wide-awake trying to figure out any way this disastrous situation could turn out well.

8

Megan sat in the kitchen with Mick's namesake on the morning after Thanksgiving and tried to coax a smile from him as she spooned one of the hastily purchased jars of baby food into his mouth. They'd been guessing about whether he was beyond just drinking formula, but the baby had eagerly seized on his first spoonful of pears as if it was a favorite.

He reminded her so much of Connor when he'd been this age that it made her heart ache. He was alert to everything going on around him. It almost felt as if she had a chance to make things right with her younger son.

Unfortunately, Connor himself was still nowhere to be found. He'd ignored all of Kevin's calls, and even those placed this morning by Mick in a fit of frustration.

"Looks just like his daddy and his granddaddy did at that age," Nell said, joining them in the kitchen. "Has to be at least nine months, don't you think?"

Megan nodded. "I'd thought at first he was a bit younger, but he's trying to pull himself up in the crib, and he's obviously used to baby food. I think I saw the beginnings of a tooth in his mouth, as well."

Nell made herself a cup of tea, then sat down at the table, smiling as the child grabbed a few Cheerios from the tray of his high chair and stuffed them into his mouth, then reached for the spoon Megan was holding. "Has their appetite, too, I see."

Megan laughed. "The men in this family have always had healthy appetites," she concurred.

Nell studied the baby. "Whatever's gone on with Connor and the child's mother, he's been well cared for. That much is clear."

"It is," Megan agreed, then gave Nell a worried look and asked yet again, "What on earth are we going to do?" She'd been so sure it would all be sorted out by this morning.

"Do as his mother asked and take care of him until we can get Connor to come to his senses, I imagine," Nell replied, her tone matter-of-fact.

"You seem to be taking this in stride," Megan noted. One of the things she'd most admired about Nell over the years was her unflappable nature. Whenever there was any kind of crisis, she was a good person to have around. Nothing seemed to faze her, not even the most outrageous foibles of her children or grandchildren. She'd been the ideal person to step in with Abby, Bree, Jess, Kevin and Connor after Megan had left. If her children couldn't be in New York with her, Megan had at least known they were well cared for here with Nell, just as Heather obviously felt her son was safe with Connor's family.

"When you've lived as long as I have, there's nothing you haven't seen," Nell replied. "Most things work out the way they're supposed to."

"Do you think Mick and I are meant to get back together?" Megan asked, unable to keep a wistful note out of her voice.

"I heard what you said to him last night about

trust," Nell said. "That's a hard thing to earn back. Obviously, for you, Mick hasn't quite done that yet."

"It's ironic, isn't it, that I'm the one who broke the trust all those years ago," Megan said. "I'm the one who turned to someone else. I might not have had an affair, but I did go looking for the attention Mick wasn't giving me. And he's forgiven me for that. It hardly seems fair that I'm withholding my forgiveness."

"Is it forgiveness you're withholding, or are you struggling to find the faith to believe that Mick's really changed?" Nell asked.

Megan thought about the question and knew her former mother-in-law had gotten it exactly right. "I guess I am having trouble believing he's changed," she admitted. "I wish I didn't feel that way."

"Feelings are what they are," Nell said. "And most of the time they're complicated, not logical. Just look at the situation with Connor and this beautiful boy of his. Even without seeing all of them together, I just know that Connor cares for them as much as if they were a real family. He's done everything right, except for taking that one step."

"Marrying Heather," Megan said.

"Exactly, and I'm guessing that Kevin got it exactly right, that it's not because Connor doesn't love her, but because he doesn't have a lot of faith in marriage."

"Because of Mick and me," Megan said with regret.

The back door opened just then and Connor walked in, looking harried and perhaps a little hungover. Baby Mick's eyes lit up at the sight of him, and a smile spread across his little face, which pretty much confirmed what everyone had suspected: Connor was his father.

"Da!" the baby shouted gleefully, holding up his arms.

Ignoring Megan and his grandmother, Connor scooped his son into his arms and held him tightly, a tear leaking from the corner of his eye, surprising his mother and grandmother. "Hey, kiddo, I didn't know you were coming for a visit," he said in what had to be the most massive understatement ever uttered in that house.

Megan studied her son's expression and saw all of the love she would have hoped for shining in his eyes as he held his boy.

His expression shut down, however, as he turned to her. "Mind telling me what happened here yesterday?" he asked, as if this were, in some way, all her fault.

"Watch your tone," Nell cautioned.

"Sorry," Connor said automatically. "I just need to understand what's going on."

"So do we," Megan replied mildly. "It seems no one in the family knew you had a son. Kevin suspected, but the rest of us didn't have a clue."

"It's complicated," Connor said, not denying that the boy was his.

"I'm pretty smart. So's your grandmother. Try us," Megan said, regarding him with an unyielding expression.

Just then Mick walked into the kitchen. "Took you long enough to get here," he declared. "You have a lot of explaining to do, young man."

Connor opened his mouth to reply, glanced at Mick, then shook his head. "Not now. I need to get him home to his mother."

"Has his mother come home then?" Mick asked.

Connor hesitated, then admitted, "I have no idea. I haven't been back there in a couple of days."

"Maybe you ought to know for sure before you take that boy anywhere," Mick said. "His mother seemed to want him to stay here. Ask *your* mother.

Heather, if that's who she is, said she wanted him here."

Connor frowned. "You saw her?" He didn't sound entirely pleased about that.

"I did," Megan said. "She didn't walk off and leave him on the doorstep with a note. And what she actually said was that he needed his father."

Connor looked relieved. "Thank heaven she didn't run off with him," he mumbled, then gave them a pleading look. "Can we please get into this later? I need to find Heather and try to sort things out. I don't know what she was thinking. The last time I saw her, she was sitting in my living room. I thought things were fine. I didn't have a clue she was thinking about taking off."

"When was that?" Megan asked.

"Day before yesterday. I was on the phone arguing with Dad. When I got off, she gave me this look that said she didn't like what was going on. I didn't want to discuss it, so I went out."

"And just stayed away?" Mick asked incredulously.

"I needed time alone to think," Connor said defensively. "I knew I wouldn't get that with Heather nagging at me to come down here for Thanksgiving."

"Yes, I can understand why you might not want to

hear that," Mick said wryly. "The woman obviously has a level head on her shoulders."

"Mick, you're not helping," Megan said quietly. "We need to get to the bottom of this."

"I think we have," Mick said. "Heather had an opinion that Connor didn't want to hear, and instead of sticking around and discussing it like a man, he walked out. Then she packed up and left, brought the baby here and has taken off. Can't say I blame her. Connor's obviously not acting responsibly these days."

"You don't know what you're talking about," Connor replied testily. "I've been responsible from the very beginning."

"Are you married?" Mick asked.

"No, but—"

"Then you haven't been responsible," Mick insisted.

Megan regarded Mick with a warning look, then turned to her son. "Connor, maybe the baby should stay right here while you find Heather and talk things over. We can look out for him."

Rather than smoothing the waters, her suggestion was greeted with anger.

"You want to dump another child on Gram to raise?" Connor asked bitterly.

"Connor!" Nell said sharply, which was enough to put a chagrined expression on his face.

"Sorry," he murmured.

"Just keep in mind that I'm not the one who dropped him off here," Megan said quietly. "And I'll stay right here for as long as it takes for you to work things out with his mother."

"Yeah, right."

Nell stood up. Even though Connor towered over her, she had him backing up a step. "Okay, that's enough, young man. You do not speak to your mother like that," she said in a voice filled with disapproval. "I taught you better than that. So did she and your father."

Connor looked for an instant as if he might argue, then nodded. "Sorry again."

"Right now this isn't about you and me," Megan said. "It's about your son. Will you leave him here for the time being?" She tried not to make it sound like the desperate plea it really was. She wasn't entirely sure why she saw this child as the answer to her prayers. Maybe, though, she could finally reach Connor through his son.

* * *

When Connor had gone off in search of Heather and the baby was napping upstairs, Mick found Megan and regarded her with frustration.

"You let that boy off the hook," he accused.

"I did no such thing. He needs to work things out with Heather before he worries about any explanations he owes us," she told him. "Try to keep the goal in mind."

"And what would that be?" he inquired testily. He'd thought it was getting things settled so he and Megan could move forward with their wedding. Something told him, though, that he'd be wise not to mention that right now.

"Getting Connor, Heather and their son back together." She gave him a wistful look. "Wouldn't it be wonderful if that happened before Christmas? I would love for all of us to celebrate the holidays together."

"Nobody would be happier about that than I would be, but Connor's a stubborn one, as you perfectly well know. Don't get your hopes up." He hesitated, then asked, "What if things don't work out between them?"

"They will eventually," she said with confidence. "I'm certain they love each other."

"And in the meantime, are you and I supposed to sit around and wait?" he asked, because he couldn't help himself. He needed to know what she had in mind for the two of them.

"Mick, I can't think about our wedding right now, if that's what you're asking."

He studied her implacable expression, then slowly nodded. "I see. I guess that tells me all I need to know."

He stood up, walked into the foyer and grabbed his coat, then walked out of the house, slamming the door behind him. Megan had found the perfect excuse for postponing their future yet again. And while he'd once thought he would wait forever to have her back, now he wondered if even that wasn't a fool's dream.

"Why did Dad just storm out of here looking like a thundercloud?" Abby asked Megan when she arrived not two minutes after Mick's departure. "He barely even acknowledged me."

Megan sighed. "He asked me a question, and he didn't like my answer," she admitted.

"About the wedding, I assume," Abby said, her expression dismayed. "You're still insisting on postponing it, aren't you?"

Megan nodded. "There really isn't any choice."

"Of course there is," Abby snapped, then studied her curiously. "Mom, do you really want to marry Dad again? I thought you loved him, but maybe you just needed to see if you could get him back. Is that it?"

Megan was genuinely shocked by the question. "Of course not! I've never stopped loving him."

"Then why are you seizing on every excuse imaginable to keep from walking down the aisle?"

"The timing has to be right," Megan replied defensively. "Not just for me, but for everyone in the family."

"Meaning Connor," Abby concluded. "Don't you think he has more on his mind these days than whether you and Dad marry again?"

"Of course he does. And we need to help him through this," Megan said.

"By postponing your own happiness?"

"I'm happy enough right now. Your father and I are together, even if we haven't remarried. I've reconciled with you, Bree, Jess and Kevin."

Abby gave her a hard look. "You know who you sound like right now? You sound like Connor. I'll bet you he's said something very much like that to Heather a thousand times over the years. He loves her, he's happy, they have it all except a ring and a marriage license, yada-yada-yada. Based on the fact that she's just walked out on him and left his son here with us, I don't think she bought it. Dad's not on board with it coming from you, either, and if you don't wake up and see that, you're going to blow it, Mom. Dad has his pride. Surely you know all about that. It's what kept him from following you when you left us."

Megan winced at the certainty she heard in Abby's voice. "Your father's not giving up on us," she said, but after the way he'd just stormed out of the house, she no longer felt quite as confident about that. "And if he does, then it wasn't meant to be."

"Oh, Mom, you know better than that. If Dad's pride kicks in and he feels as if you're going to keep finding excuse after excuse to postpone the wedding, he'll walk away."

Megan knew that Abby had a point, but she couldn't allow herself to be bullied into agreeing to a wedding date just because Mick had all but uttered an ultimatum. Besides, it hadn't come to that yet. He might be frustrated. He might even be annoyed. But he wasn't going to throw in the towel, at least not yet.

"Your father and I will work this out," she assured Abby. "I promise."

Abby regarded her skeptically. "I hope so, Mom, for your sake, because I don't know if you'll ever be truly happy if you blow this chance with Dad."

Though she wasn't about to admit it aloud, Megan wondered about that, as well.

At loose ends after walking out on Megan, Mick eventually made his way to Sally's. To his surprise, he found both Kevin and Connor already there. He scowled at his younger son.

"I thought you were supposed to be off making things right with Heather."

"I would be, if I could find her," Connor admitted, sounding thoroughly frustrated. "She's not answering her cell, and no one I've called will admit to knowing where she is."

"Probably serves you right," Mick muttered, sliding in next to Kevin and ordering coffee and a slice of warm apple pie with ice cream on top.

Connor frowned at him. "Gee, thanks for the support, Dad."

Mick was about to reply, but Kevin stepped in before they could start a full-scale argument. "Why are you here looking as if you lost your best friend?" he asked Mick. "I thought you liked to spend every minute with Mom when she came to town."

"Your mother and I aren't seeing eye to eye at the moment," Mick admitted.

Connor's expression brightened. "Have you given up your plan to marry her?" he inquired hopefully. "I've known from the beginning it was a bad idea. It's about time you saw the light."

"You don't know anything," Mick retorted. "We'll get married, but it might not be on the timetable I had in mind."

Kevin frowned. "Why not? I thought a New Year's Eve wedding had been all but carved in stone."

Just as Sally set down his coffee and pie, Mick cast a pointed look in Connor's direction. "Your mother seems to think we'll never be happy if Connor can't accept the two of us being back together. She also doesn't think we should get married while his life's in turmoil."

Connor regarded him with disbelief. "So this is one more thing that's my fault?"

"Just telling it like it is," Mick said, jabbing his fork into the pie and spearing a large chunk of apple dripping with melted vanilla ice cream. "Your mother wants us all to be one big happy family, and until that happens, she's not on board with the wedding."

"You do realize that getting everyone in this family happy at the same time is like trying to herd cats, don't you?" Connor said. "There are too many of us. Life happens. Things go wrong. People fight."

"Well, all of that has to stop," Mick declared. "I mean it. I want this wedding and, by God, nothing is going to stand in its way!" He scowled at Connor. "Especially not you."

"Hey, I have my own problems to worry about," Connor protested. "You're on your own with Mom."

"If only that were true," Mick grumbled.

Kevin held up a hand. "Okay, hold on here. If Mom wants Connor to be happy, then let's take a step back and focus on him for a minute. Connor, do you have any more ideas about where Heather might have gone? Did you try her family?"

Connor winced. "They're not very happy with either of us. They didn't approve of our decision to have the baby without getting married. I doubt Heather would have gone running to them. If nothing else, she wouldn't want to admit she'd left their grandchild behind with me."

"Is there a place she liked to go off to when she wanted to think?" Kevin persisted. "Maybe the beach or the mountains, any place like that?"

Connor shook his head.

"How well do you even know this woman?" Mick asked. "You don't seem to have any clue about her habits."

"I know Heather as well as you know Mom," Connor claimed.

"Now, why would you say a thing like that?" Mick demanded. "I know your mother better than any other person on this earth."

"You apparently didn't know how miserable she was when you were married," Connor suggested. "Or did you just ignore all the signs?"

Mick bristled, but he couldn't deny Connor's guesswork. He had known Megan was unhappy back then. He just hadn't believed she would ever leave him. "I made my share of mistakes, and turning a blind eye to her unhappiness was at the top of the list," he admitted to his sons. "Which is why I'm here to tell you to learn from them. If you love this woman, then you need to figure out the things that matter to her."

"Oh, I know what matters to Heather," Connor said bleakly. "She wants to get married. She told me she didn't. She swore to me she understood how I felt about marriage. Even after she got pregnant, she claimed she was okay with us just living together and being a family. She said all the right things, exactly what I wanted to hear." He sighed heavily. "But she didn't mean a word of it."

Mick looked in his son's eyes and saw the pain and confusion there. It was something to which he could relate. Megan had often told him what he needed to hear at the time, and he'd been too full of himself to see it for the attempt it was just to keep peace between them during the rare time they had together back then.

"So, how are you going to fix this, son?" he asked Connor. "Do you know what you're going to say once you've found her? What you're going to do?"

Connor shook his head. "Not a clue, to be honest. I can't back down on the stance I've taken. That's who I am, what I believe."

"And that means more to you than she does, than keeping your family together?" Mick pressed.

Connor nodded, but he looked less certain. Like way too many of the O'Briens, he clearly wanted to have things his own way, even if that way was selfish and shortsighted.

"You'd rather lose her than bend?" Kevin asked, regarding his brother incredulously. "If there's one thing I know about marriage, it's that it involves give-and-take. Both people need to compromise."

"Getting married when I don't believe in it wouldn't just be bending or compromising," Connor insisted. "It would be going against my own principles."

"A noble stance," Kevin said. "But I guarantee it won't keep your bed warm at night, and it will assure that you see your son only on holidays and the occasional weekend. You're a divorce lawyer. You know how things like this go."

"There's no divorce involved," Connor said. "We were never married."

Kevin shook his head. "You say that as if it simplifies everything. Doesn't it actually make the whole custody thing even trickier? What kind of legal claim do you have to that boy? Is your name even on the birth certificate?"

"Of course it is." Connor scowled at him. "Whose side are you on?"

"Yours always," Kevin said. "Except when you're being too pigheaded to admit what you really want."

"I want Heather and my boy back home," Connor said emphatically.

"But only on your terms," Kevin said. He glanced at Mick and raised his cup of coffee in a mocking toast. "And isn't that the O'Brien way?"

Mick sighed heavily. "It is, indeed."

Something told him he and his son needed to find a new way, or they were both going to lose the most important people in their lives.

9

Ever since he'd seen his father, baby Mick had turned fussy. Clearly he'd tired of unfamiliar faces and wanted his mommy or his daddy back. Megan was at her wit's end. She'd paced the floor with him. Nell had found some of Davy's colorful toys and rattles in the attic and brought those down, but the baby wasn't interested.

"He's probably teething," Nell concluded. "I'll get something cold for his gums."

Unfortunately that didn't work, either. He just

screwed up his little face and cried harder. Finally, in desperation, Megan called Connor.

"You need to get back to the house," she said when he answered.

"Why? Giving up already on babysitting?"

"Save the sarcasm," she said. "Your son needs to see a familiar face. Since I can't reach his mother and I can find you, you're the one who needs to step up." The baby let out another howl just then, as if to echo her point.

"I'll be right there," Connor said with surprising alacrity. He hesitated, then added, "In the meantime, if you could sing to him, it might help. He likes that when Heather does it, not so much when I do. I can't carry a tune, and he clearly objects to that. He's probably a budding music critic."

Megan chuckled. "You know, you were exactly the same way," she reminded him. "You loved it when your father or I sang, but let Abby or Bree try to calm you that way and you screamed so loudly you drowned them out."

Connor was silent, perhaps surprised that she remembered anything about his childhood. "I'll be there in a few minutes," he said eventually.

Satisfied that he was on his way, Megan cuddled

the baby against her shoulder and walked around the house singing "When Irish Eyes Are Smiling." It had been Connor's favorite, better than any lullaby. Amazingly, the baby settled right down in her arms.

"Ah, these O'Briens," she murmured. "Ireland's in their blood, no matter how far removed they are from Dublin."

Back upstairs as she put the now-sleeping baby into his crib, she heard Connor sprinting up the stairs.

"He's asleep," he whispered in surprise when he walked into the room.

"Singing worked like a charm," Megan told him. "I'm sorry I made you come back here for no reason. I just felt so awful for him being alone in a strange place."

"It's okay. I think I needed a glimpse of him, anyway." Connor sighed heavily as he stood looking down at his son. He brushed a finger gently over the boy's cheek. "He's beautiful, isn't he?"

"He looks exactly like you did at that age," Megan told him.

Connor regarded her skeptically. "Don't all grandmothers say that?"

"Only if it's true. If I had your baby book here, I could prove it to you."

Connor frowned. "Where is it? I haven't seen it in years. I figured it was stuffed in some box in the attic."

Megan shook her head. "It's in New York, along with all the others."

"You took our baby books with you?"

She nodded. "Looking at them gave me comfort. They also reminded me of what I'd left behind. I also kept scrapbooks of clippings for each of you, along with all the pictures Gram and your father sent after I'd gone. Someday I'll return them to all of you, so you can show them to your children. Your whole lives are summed up in those albums and in your school yearbooks. I have those, too."

Connor looked as if he didn't know what to make of her sentimental actions. "I had no idea," he murmured.

"No idea about what?" she asked. "That I'd missed you? Of course I did. You're my children, Connor. I had so many memories stored in my heart, but they weren't nearly enough. Not a day went by that I didn't yearn for a glimpse of each of you. I craved news about what you were doing. I missed the days when you'd come running into the kitchen after school to grab a glass of milk and a handful of cookies and tell me about your day."

She smiled at him. "I remember the first time you mentioned a girl and I knew you had your first crush. I also remember when she broke your heart by going to a Valentine's party with someone else. I think you were eleven."

"Twelve," he corrected, grinning. "Jennifer McGee. She was something! She had the most beautiful blond hair I'd ever seen. More important, she could hit a baseball a country mile. That impressed the daylights out of me."

Megan laughed. "I remember."

His expression sobered. "Heather played on the girl's softball team in high school. By college, though, she'd given it up to be a cheerleader. She still had a good eye, though. She probably should have been a coach or something. She helped me with my game almost as much as the team coach did." He looked startled for a moment, as if he'd just realized something. "Isn't it funny that it was baseball that drew me to Jennifer when I was just a kid and then to Heather? They even looked a little bit alike. I had no idea I had a type when it came to women."

"You shouldn't be so surprised," Megan told him.

"You've always been consistent about the things that matter to you." She grinned at him. "Some might even say stubborn. I assume there are other things you love about Heather now that you've gotten to know her."

For a moment she thought he might not reveal anything more about his innermost feelings, but then he said softly, his gaze on his son, "She's the calmest woman I know. She reminds me of Gram in that way. I feel at peace when I'm with her, at least until lately. Lately all we do is argue."

"About getting married?"

He shook his head, surprising her. "Not really. I know that's something she wants, but she doesn't throw it in my face every five minutes. In fact, she doesn't mention it at all."

"What, then?"

He glanced at her, then turned away before admitting, "She thinks I've been too hard on you. And she was furious when I refused to come home for Thanksgiving."

"If you'd come, would you have brought her?" Megan asked.

Connor was silent for a long time, then shook his head. "I wasn't ready to spring her on everyone and try to explain our relationship and the baby. To be honest, I think that's why I felt relieved when Dad ordered me to stay away. I was hurt, sure, but what I really felt most of all was relief that I wouldn't have to deal with all of this yet. I've been putting it off so long it's gotten to be a habit. A bad one, I know."

Megan hesitated, then dared to put her hand over his on the side of the crib. "Oh, Connor, secrets have a way of making things so much more complicated than they need to be. Did you really have so little faith that we would understand or at least try to accept your relationship?"

He gave her an incredulous look. "You have to be kidding! Dad doesn't understand anything, just as I anticipated. Kevin's done nothing but give me grief. I expect to be hearing from Abby, Bree and Jess before long." He hesitated then added, "The only one who hasn't gone on about this is actually you."

"Because I just want to understand," she said. "And maybe because I blame myself for the way you feel about marriage. Isn't that why you're so conflicted in the first place?"

"That's part of it, and then I see marriages unraveling every single day at work. People who supposedly loved each other get angry and bitter and downright nasty, and I'm the one who has to fight for what's fair for my client without allowing myself to think for even a second about what's fair to the other person or to the kids. Even though I hated that you left, at least you and Dad never battled over everything. Back then, I was furious with him for giving you so much without a fight, but now I see how much better it was for us that you kept things civilized."

"Do you know what I regret about that?" she said. "Mick and I were so busy being civilized and trying to make things easier that you, your brother and your sisters apparently decided that I didn't care enough to fight for you. You all came to the conclusion, I think, that I was happy to be rid of you, when nothing could have been further from the truth."

"I guess it's easy to misjudge a situation when you don't know all the facts, isn't it?" he said, looking uncomfortable at the admission.

"It is," she agreed, then hugged him. "But we're correcting that now, Connor. We've made a start."

And with any luck, they would find their way back to the easy, loving relationship they'd once had. It would just take time. She was willing to wait forever, if necessary, but she knew that Mick had far less patience.

* * *

On Sunday night, Mick insisted that he, Connor and Megan sit down after supper to discuss how to handle having the baby in the house.

"I won't have Ma burdened with trying to baby-sit," he said flatly.

Unfortunately he said it just as Nell walked into the kitchen. "Are you saying I'm to old to care for a baby, Mick O'Brien?" she demanded.

He flinched under her scrutiny. "Of course not, Ma, but babysitting's one thing. Full-time care is another. I'm just saying it's Connor's responsibility to figure this out."

"Well, I can certainly pitch in," Nell said.

"Of course you can," Megan soothed. "And I will, as well."

"No," Connor said. "Dad's right. This is my responsibility. I've already spoken to Abby, and their nanny can look after little Mick, at least for a few days. I'll drop him off there before I go to Baltimore for work in the morning."

"And who'll care for him at night?" Mick asked. "I know the kind of hours you work. Are you planning on leaving him over at Abby's all day and into the night?"

Connor sighed. "I'll figure out someway to get out of the office and back down here by dinner. Hopefully I'll track Heather down soon and we can work this out. This arrangement won't have to go on indefinitely."

Mick looked at Megan and saw the determined set of her jaw. She clearly wasn't happy with the plan. "Megan, you have another idea?"

She nodded. "Nell, if it's okay with you, I'm going to fly up to New York first thing in the morning, take care of a few things at the gallery and come back at the end of the day. If you can care for the baby tomorrow, I'll be back to take over. Connor, I'll keep the baby right here for you until you and Heather have worked things out. He's just now adjusting to being here with us. It doesn't make sense to shuffle him off to Abby's to a nanny he doesn't know."

Mick regarded her with surprise. "You're going to quit your job now?" he inquired hopefully. It was what he'd wanted for a long time now.

"It's the only thing that makes sense," she conceded. "It was only a matter of weeks before I quit anyway. I'm needed here now, that is if Connor doesn't have any objections."

"Why would he?" Mick demanded, scowling at his son. "You're bailing him out of a jam."

"I'm helping out in a family emergency," Megan corrected. "Connor, is this okay with you?"

"I don't know what to say," he said eventually. "I didn't expect you to do something like this."

Megan gave him a sad look. "Perhaps because you don't expect much of me at all. Let me do this, Connor. I'd love to spend time with the baby, and if I can make this easier for you at the same time, I'm happy to do it."

Mick recognized that his son was caught between a rock and a hard place. He obviously knew this was the best offer he was likely to get. At the same time, it solidified Megan's role in all of their lives and made it much more likely that there would be a wedding soon. Mick was ecstatic, but he understood why Connor was hesitating. For once, he kept silent, trusting his son to make the only reasonable choice.

Even though he looked torn, Connor finally nodded. "Thank you, Mom. It's a very generous offer, and I'd really appreciate knowing the baby is in at least somewhat familiar surroundings, with people who'll love him. Gram, I can take him over to Abby's for tomorrow, if having him here will be too much for you."

"Nonsense," Nell said. "He'll stay here with me."

"Okay, then," Megan said. "Let me go upstairs and make some phone calls. I need to put some things in order before I break the news to Phillip in the morning."

"You could just call him," Mick suggested. "Explain on the phone."

Megan shook her head. "No, I owe it to him to tell him in person, and I'll be able to organize my work at the gallery so someone else can step in or I can handle it from here for the time being. Plus, I'll need to pack more clothes if I'm going to be down here indefinitely."

"You're going to be here permanently," Mick corrected.

Megan gave him an inscrutable look. "Possibly. If that turns out to be the case, I'll eventually have to close my apartment and have all of my things shipped down here, but we don't have time to deal with that now."

Mick dropped the subject. The most important thing was that this unexpected twist with Connor was bringing Megan back to Chesapeake Shores for the foreseeable future. That should give him plenty of time to convince her that a New Year's Eve wedding was still in the cards.

Megan dreaded the conversation she was about to have with Phillip. For all of his faults, and there were many, he'd given her a chance years ago and trained her for a career in art that she'd come to love. Abandoning him with virtually no notice was not the way she'd wanted to handle things.

When she arrived at the Upper East Side gallery at 10:00 a.m. Monday, she was carrying two large lattes and wearing a penitent expression. Phillip was in the back, uncrating a painting that would be the centerpiece of their next show. By a new modern artist, it was bold and stunning. Megan regarded it with awe.

"That ought to sell the minute we open the doors," she said. "Are the rest of his works half as good?"

"Of course, or I wouldn't be giving him a solo show," Phillip said, accepting his coffee, then taking a second look at her. "What's wrong?"

"I have some news," she said. "I don't think you're going to be very happy about it."

"Mick's convinced you to move back to Chesapeake Shores immediately to get ready for the wedding," he said, looking resigned.

Megan regarded him with wonder. "Are you psychic, or just highly intuitive? I do need to move back to Chesapeake Shores right away, but it's not about Mick." She explained about the weekend's events. "This is my chance to do something for my son and maybe make peace with him in the process."

Phillip looked stunned. "You're going home to play granny?"

Megan frowned at his characterization. "I'm not going to be playing anything. I *am* a grandmother."

"Megan, it was one thing when you said you were going to marry Mick and open your own art gallery. That's all about the man you've always loved and a career you're passionate about. *This*—glorified babysitting—it's just not you. How can I let you do it?"

"You don't really have a choice," she said tightly. "It's my decision. I will do whatever I can today to help you find a replacement and leave things in order for him or her, but I'm going back home tonight, Phillip. That's final."

"I think you're going to regret it," he declared. "And what about your gallery? And the wedding?"

"In due time," she said evasively.

He scowled at her answer. "Meaning you've put them on hold?"

"Only temporarily," she insisted.

"And what does Mick have to say about this? He doesn't strike me as a patient man."

"He doesn't have a say," she said, then realized just how much she sounded exactly like Mick. She, too, seemed to be making decisions without regard for the man she claimed to love.

Phillip looked as startled by her response as she was. "And how does he feel about that?"

She sighed. "No better than I do when he does the same thing to me," she admitted. "But that's another reason I need to be in Chesapeake Shores. If things are going to work out for us, we need to figure out a better way to communicate. Right now we both seem to be issuing a lot of edicts."

Phillip's gaze narrowed. "Trouble in paradise?"

She frowned at the hopeful note in his voice. "Stop it. Mick and I will get married."

"We'll see," Phillip responded.

He left the room whistling, which was so annoying Megan almost picked up her purse and walked out. Unfortunately, a deeply ingrained sense of responsibility kept her where she was.

A few more hours of dealing with him after all he'd done for her was the least she could do.

And then she'd be back in Chesapeake Shores with the other irritating males in her life.

Mick spent Monday impatiently awaiting Megan's return. He was underfoot so much, his mother finally lost patience.

"You need something to do," Nell declared. "Go up in the attic and bring down the Christmas decorations."

"It's not even the first of December yet," he protested.

"Doesn't matter. It will keep you out of my way. Besides, you know how long it takes to get this house decorated. Even if you start outside this afternoon, it'll be days before you finish."

"I thought Jake was going to put up all the outside lights," Mick grumbled. "Didn't his landscape company start doing that a couple of years back? Let him climb up and down ladders. I don't need to do it. Besides, we need to support his business so he has money to provide for that baby he and Bree are expecting."

Nell stood in the kitchen, hands on her hips, her

expression exasperated. "Do you really want to argue with me about this? Even if Jake does the work, he still has to have the decorations. They're in the attic. Bring them down."

Mick turned on his heel and left. "Bossy old woman," he muttered under his breath.

"I heard that," she called after him. "You're not too old for me to wash your mouth out with soap."

"I'd like to see you try," Mick shouted back, laughing.

"Don't you tempt me, Michael Devlin O'Brien," she retorted, though there was amusement threading through her voice, as well. "And if you wake the baby with all this commotion, you'll be the one pacing the floor with him."

Taking the threat seriously, Mick crept up the stairs as quietly as he could. He'd barely reached the second-floor landing, though, when the crying started. With a sigh of resignation, he walked into Connor's room.

"Did Grandpa wake you up?" he murmured, picking the boy up and cradling him against his chest, then wincing. "Or was it this soggy diaper?"

He made quick work of changing the baby, then took note of the fact that he appeared to be wide-awake. "How about you and me spend a little guy time together?" he said. "You can come up in the attic and help me sort through the decorations."

The baby gurgled happily at the suggestion.

Mick put him in his carrier, then climbed up to the attic. One step inside, he knew this was going to be no simple task. His mother had been right about that.

One of these days he was actually going to organize the mess up here. Every year he vowed to put all of the Christmas decorations away in an orderly fashion, and every year things got stuffed into boxes then shoved into whatever corner of the room happened to be empty. Usually half the boxes he carted downstairs turned out not to have a single decoration inside, because no one had ever bothered to mark anything.

"Looks as if we have our work cut out for us," he told the baby as he settled the carrier on top of a large, stable box which would give him a view of the room as Mick worked. He spotted an old CD player nearby, then found the box of Christmas CDs that was stored up here. He popped one in, and music filled the attic. "A little mood music," he told the baby as Johnny Mathis sang about chestnuts roasting. "Now, that was a man who knew how to sing."

Even as Mick spoke, the baby's eyes drifted shut. It was pretty amazing how easily soothed he was by a good voice and a lovely old song.

With the baby settled, Mick started opening boxes to check out the contents, moving those with actual decorations closer to the door. Several of the boxes contained only the massive number of strands of lights for outdoors. He plugged them in one by one, discarding those that didn't work. It was a tedious task, but it gave him time to think about how different this holiday season would be with a new baby in the house and Megan practically home for good.

Perhaps it had something to do with his nostalgic mood, but when he came to the box of ornaments the kids had made when they were small, he sat down to look through them. Each one stirred a memory, beginning with a more or less tree-shaped ornament made of clay that Abby had painted bright green then dotted with colored lumps of clay to represent the ornaments. She'd been five, as he recalled, and in kindergarten. Bree's lopsided angel was next, the wings askew. Next he found Kevin's attempt at a clay puppy, a less than subtle hint that he'd wanted a dog that year. He'd tied a red ribbon around the dog's neck in place of a collar.

Connor's first ornament, made apparently in preschool, was simply a handprint in a blob of clay. It had been painted a festive shade of red.

Last he came upon Jess's attempt. Even then she'd struggled with her attention deficit disorder. Her Santa's hat, if that's what it was, had a streak of white paint and another streak of red, but little else in the way of detail. She'd obviously tired of the project. Her name had been carefully printed on the back, though, most likely by the teacher.

Mick tried to recall the moment the children had presented these ornaments to him and Megan, but he couldn't. Something told him he hadn't been around to see the pride shining in their eyes or to add his words of praise to Megan's. How many moments of their lives had he missed because of work? Most of the big ones, he was certain of that much. No wonder Megan had lost patience with him.

Now, though, he would get it right. His grandchildren would know they were loved. And it wasn't too late to show his children how much they mattered, as well. Most of all, though, he would prove to Megan that he could be the devoted, attentive husband she deserved.

But first he had to get her in front of a minister on New Year's Eve. And given her stubborn resistance to the idea, that was going to be easier said than done.

10

Megan had forgotten how tiring it was to care for an infant. By midafternoon when the baby went down for his nap, she was out for the count, as well. She was asleep on the sofa in the den, when she felt someone gently place a blanket over her. She stirred and glanced up into Mick's worried eyes.

"I was trying not to wake you," he said ruefully. "Go back to sleep. You're worn-out."

She sat up and rubbed her eyes. "No, I need to get up. I should be using this time to get a few things done in the living room. All those decorations you carted downstairs should be sorted out and put where they belong, so we're ready when we pick out the tree. When are we doing that, by the way? You and I could go this weekend."

"It's too soon," Mick protested. "It'll be dead by Christmas."

She smiled at his response. "You used to say that every year. The kids and I were always so impatient to get a tree into the house, and you always insisted we wait. I think it was so you wouldn't have to go with us and listen to us debate the merits of every tree on the lot." She gave him a defiant look. "Well, this year I'm not waiting. Having a tree will perk up everyone's spirits. We can have the whole family over one evening to help us decorate it."

Mick relented. "Sure. If that's what you want."

"It is." She threw off the blanket and stood. "Now I'd better get those boxes sorted out. Most go to the living room, but I'm almost certain some of those things belong in the dining room and some in the foyer. I might as well get them out of here." She nodded toward the stack of boxes sitting in the middle of the floor.

"That doesn't have to be done right this minute," Mick argued. "Lie back down and get some rest while you can. If the baby wakes up, I'll get him. He and I are buddies now. We have things to do."

She regarded him with amusement. "Such as?"

"Well, today I thought we'd go into town and do a little shopping."

Megan stared at him incredulously. "You're going to take the baby Christmas shopping?"

"I've already put the stroller and car seat that Connor brought last night into the car. I thought the baby would like to see all the lights and the store windows," he said. "The other kids have already been. He shouldn't be left out."

"I doubt he's aware that he's been left out," she said wryly.

"It's the principle," Mick insisted.

She eyed him with amusement. "Admit it, Mick. You just want a chance to show him off at Sally's, don't you? That's what this is really about."

Mick shrugged. "So what if it is?"

"How cold is it outside?"

"I have no idea. What's that got to do with anything?"

"If you're going to take the baby into town, he needs to be dressed for the weather. And then he needs to take off some of those things while you're in Sally's so he doesn't get too warm. I'll come with you," she concluded decisively. She met Mick's gaze. "Unless you have some objection to me coming along?"

Mick's eyes brightened at once. "Of course not. It'll be like the old days."

She regarded him with amusement. "What old days would those be?"

"When we took the kids to see the lights."

"Mick O'Brien, you were never once here to go traipsing around town looking at the holiday decorations," she reminded him. "You generally breezed in on Christmas Eve, tugged on a Santa outfit, said ho-ho-ho a few times, passed out presents and went to bed."

"I most certainly did not," he retorted indignantly. "How'd all those toys get assembled for Christmas morning?"

"Most of the time, if I couldn't put them together myself, I threw myself on the mercy of some neighbor who was handy with a screwdriver," she recalled. "The one exception was the dollhouse you made for the girls. You built that yourself. I never did figure out how you found the time when you were away so much."

It was a beautiful Victorian structure with every tiny detail carefully crafted. She'd been as awed as the girls had been.

"I think it was their most prized possession," she told him. "It was the one thing they never minded sharing. They brought all of their friends over to see what their dad had made for them. They had bragging rights over owning an original Mick O'Brien architectural design, even if it was on a small scale."

Mick looked momentarily taken aback. "I'd forgotten all about that. Where is it now? The twins should have it."

"They do," Megan reminded him. "Trace took it over to their house a few months ago. If Bree has a girl, Abby's promised to pass it on to her when the twins outgrow playing with it. I suppose Jess's children will eventually have it, too."

Mick sighed. "I missed too much, didn't I? I built that house, but I don't think I ever saw them play with it."

"You missed some of the best times," Megan agreed. "But you won't do that now. Our grandchildren are giving both of us a second chance."

"That they are," he agreed, then regarded her with

a concerned expression. "Speaking of Jess, do you worry about her?" he asked unexpectedly.

She frowned at the question. "Why would you ask that? She's doing really well with the inn."

"No question about that, but running that place shouldn't be all she has," he complained. "It's a career. She needs a man in her life. She needs those children you were talking about. Abby, Bree and Kevin are settled now. Even Connor has someone he cares about, plus that little guy upstairs. Jess is alone. She's never stuck with anyone for long. I worry about her."

"She'll find someone when the time is right," Megan said with confidence. "In fact, I've always thought..."

"What?"

"Never mind," she said, thinking of Will Lincoln and the way he always regarded Jess with such longing in his eyes. Megan had been gone when Jess and Will were teenagers, but she had a gut feeling he'd had a crush on Jess all those years he'd been hanging around the house with Connor and Kevin. Now that they were all grown-up, though, he'd done nothing about it. Or perhaps he had, and Jess had rejected him. Megan had no way of knowing. Planting the idea in Mick's head right now, she suspected, could lead to awkward consequences. He was bound to start meddling. Knowing Jess, that would be counterproductive.

"Just trust Jess to know when the right man comes along," she told Mick.

"I want to see them all settled and happy," Mick said. "I know we're already well on our way, but I want this house filled with grandbabies."

"I know. So do I."

He gave her a pointed look. "I wouldn't mind grabbing a little of that happiness for the two of us, as well."

Megan laughed at the less than subtle reminder. "We will," she promised him. "In due time." She wrapped her arms around him. "Besides, I'm happy right now just being here with you with the holidays right around the corner. We're going to have a wonderful Christmas, Mick."

"I suppose," he said, clearly unhappy with her response and the lack of any mention of what the new year might bring.

"Mick," she said, holding his gaze. "I do love you."

"So you say," he grumbled.

"I could prove it," she suggested seductively.

To her astonishment a gleam lit Mick's eyes, but his words weren't at all what she expected.

"Not until there's a ring on your finger," he declared, looking pleased with himself.

Megan chuckled. She knew him too well to believe the threat for a single second.

"No, I mean it," he insisted. "Not until you make an honest man of me."

It was definitely a twist Megan hadn't anticipated, and it upped the stakes for getting Connor's life on track in a very big hurry.

Everyone at Sally's was fussing over the baby when Lawrence Riley walked in. The banker headed straight for Mick and Megan. He leaned down for a closer look at the baby.

"Who have we here?" he asked, returning the baby's mostly toothless smile.

"This is my namesake," Mick said proudly. "He's Connor's boy."

"I definitely recognize those O'Brien genes," Lawrence said. He straightened, then glanced at Megan, his expression sobering. "I was going to give you a call this afternoon."

Beside Mick, Megan stilled. "Oh?"

"The loan committee met this morning," he said.

"And?" Mick prodded. "Don't drag it out, man. She got the loan, right?"

Lawrence shook his head. "I'm so sorry, Megan. I thought this would go differently. I'm afraid in this economy, the committee was concerned it might be a bad time to open a small business, especially one dealing in high-end art."

Mick couldn't believe his ears. "Even after I…" His voice trailed off as he caught Megan's horrified expression.

"Mick O'Brien, did you interfere in this?" she demanded.

"I went to see Lawrence, that's all," he said hurriedly. He scowled at his longtime friend. "He assured me you had nothing to worry about, so I backed off. Now he's saying they turned you down, despite me being very clear that I was willing to back you."

Lawrence flushed guiltily. "Like I said, I'm sorry. Maybe at a later time, Megan."

Megan ignored the apology and whirled on Mick, her scowl deepening. "Mick, I told you very clearly that I didn't want you involved."

"Well, apparently that didn't work out so well," Mick retorted. "If you'd let me write the check in the first place, you'd be starting a business in a few months instead of having to scramble for other financing. I can still do that. Let Lawrence and that band of shortsighted number crunchers of his eat their hearts out when you make a huge success of this without them."

Megan shook her head. "I can't do that. If they don't think my plan is solid, then why would I take money from you and put it at risk?"

"Because this is your dream, dammit!" Mick said so forcefully that the baby began to cry.

Megan immediately stood, took the baby from his carrier and walked off, crooning softly to him.

Mick turned on Lawrence. "Are you in charge at that bank or not?"

"I don't make unilateral decisions," Lawrence said. "I'm truly sorry about this, Mick, but in this economy we've survived by being prudent. Megan has a good business plan. Maybe in a few months or another year, we can take another look at this." He regarded Mick with regret. "If you'd cosigned, it would be different, but that's not what she wanted. In fact, she was adamant about it."

Mick knew there was no point in arguing. He even understood that Megan's own stubbornness was what had cost her the financing for the gallery. That didn't make it any easier when he saw the disappointment she was covering with her anger at him.

Worse than that, it was one more blow to their future. Without that business to give her the independence she craved, it was even less likely that Megan would stay here in town.

He drew in a deep breath and resolved not to let this latest hurdle stand in their way. He had no idea how to fix this, but he would. It used to be that all the challenges in his life that mattered to him were work-related. Now he had a huge one in his personal life, and it was clearly the most important challenge he'd ever faced.

Megan wandered around Sally's holding the whimpering baby and trying not to cry herself. Her dream had just gone up in smoke, and she hadn't even seen it coming. She'd been so sure the bank would back her. It wasn't as if she'd been asking for a fortune, just enough capital for the first couple of years.

As for Mick, as annoying as his interference had been, it hadn't been unexpected. Butting in was just what he did. She couldn't really blame him for wanting to help her. At the same time, she couldn't allow it, either.

She waited until she saw Lawrence leave before returning to the table.

"We'll fix this business about the loan," Mick said at once, regarding her worriedly. "It's a setback, Meggie. Nothing more."

"Don't minimize it, Mick. If a bank that's known me for years turns down my loan application, I can't imagine that another bank will view it more favorably."

"There's still me," he said. "I believe in you, and I have the money."

She regarded him with exasperation. "How many ways do I need to say no?"

He looked as if he was ready to argue, but then he backed down. "The offer's there if you change your mind. In the meantime, what's your next step?"

"I don't have one," she admitted. "To be honest, I'm still reeling a little bit. I was so sure...." She shrugged. "I guess nothing's a sure thing these days."

"What about the partnership with Phillip you mentioned a while back?"

"I suppose that's still an option," she said, though she dreaded going back to Phillip to detail one more glitch in her plan to move to Chesapeake Shores and open her own gallery. He'd probably use it as yet another reason why she should be staying put in New York with an established business.

"You don't sound as if you like it, though," Mick said, being surprisingly perceptive.

"I don't. All the reasons I had for wanting to do this on my own are still valid. Even Phillip, though he was willing to work out a partnership arrangement, thought I'd be happier knowing I had total control."

"Is that because the two of you don't see eye to eye?" Mick asked. "Or are you afraid he'd strip you of all your authority to make decisions?"

"More than likely, that's exactly what he'd do," she admitted. "Even though we've always worked well together, I've always known he was the boss and that his decisions were final. I doubt we could change that balance of power now."

"What about—"

Before Mick could finish his thought, she cut him off. "Can we please not talk about this right now? I honestly have no idea what comes next and I'm too upset right this second to think about it."

Mick nodded. "As long as you know I'm right here

and will do whatever it takes to help you make this come together."

"I do know that, Mick, and I appreciate your faith in me more than you could possibly know." She hesitated, then said, "Can we go home now? Suddenly the last thing I want to do is wander around looking at Christmas displays. It's too cold outside for the baby, anyway."

Mick studied her worriedly. "Why don't you take the baby on home? I have a few things I'd like to do as long as I'm already in town."

"How will you get home?"

"I can still walk, can't I?" he said, sounding annoyed. "But if I don't think I can make it, I'm sure one of the many people I know in this town will give me a lift."

"Fine," she said, matching his testy tone. She regarded him with suspicion. "You're not going to the bank, are you?"

"I said everything I wanted to say to Lawrence when he was right here," Mick assured her. "Even I have sense enough not to beat a dead horse."

"Okay, then," Megan said, putting the baby back into his warm jacket and wrapping his blanket securely around him. "I'll see you at home."

Mick walked outside with her, then waited while she settled the baby into his car seat. After she'd gotten behind the wheel, Mick held her door open.

"Meggie, are you sure you're okay to drive? You still look upset."

"I'm fine," she insisted. "The house isn't even two miles away. Even if I were hysterical, which I'm not, I could probably make it that far."

"I just worry about you," Mick said.

She blinked back the tears that were threatening. "I know," she whispered, then dared to meet his gaze. "Please don't. It just makes it worse, somehow."

"Why?" he asked, clearly bewildered.

"I just don't think I can take your pity right now, or that look in your eye that tells me you're already fretting that this is just one more thing that will keep us from getting married."

"Will it?" he asked pointedly.

"It might," she conceded. "I just don't know. Let me go, Mick. I need to think and I can't do it with you hovering, however well-meant it is."

He closed the door gently then and backed away from the car. But if anything, the worried frown on his face only deepened as she drove away. She wondered how much more concerned he would have been, if he'd seen her tears start to fall.

An hour later, when Bree, Jess and Abby all arrived at the house within minutes of each other, Megan knew she had Mick to thank for the rallying of the troops. Nell immediately appeared with a pot of freshly brewed tea and a plate of still-warm, homemade cranberry-orange scones. Since she usually baked first thing in the morning, Megan gathered she'd had an emergency call, as well.

"I don't suppose this is just a coincidence," Megan said, not sure whether to laugh or cry.

"Dad stopped by the flower shop," Bree admitted.

"And the inn," Jess said.

"He called me," Abby said. "Thank goodness I was working from home today, instead of being in Baltimore."

Megan shook her head. "Did he give you instructions on what you were supposed to do?"

"Cheer you up," Abby said at once.

Bree dragged out her catalogs of flower arrangements. "I thought we could continue that discussion about flowers for the wedding. Wedding talk always cheered me up, when Jake and I were planning ours."

She whipped a small bouquet of lilies of the valley out from behind her. "I even made this up to show you. What do you think?"

"I think it's lovely," Megan said honestly. "It's much simpler and closer to what I had in mind." Still, she was not about to be drawn any further into wedding talk. "I propose we focus on your baby shower," she said instead.

Bree frowned. "The baby's not due for months. The wedding—"

"Is on hold," Megan said flatly.

Abby and Jess exchanged a look. Surprisingly, it was Jess who spoke. "Mom, it seems to me that this is the perfect time for you and Dad to go ahead with your plans."

Megan stared at her incredulously. "Perfect? With Connor and me barely starting to get along, the mother of his child missing and my plan for opening a business in utter disarray? Sweetie, I love you, but this is no time to go all mushy and romantic. I need to be realistic. How can I possibly think about getting married now?"

"Do you love Dad?" Jess demanded.

"Of course."

"Do you want to marry him?" Bree asked.

"When the time is right, absolutely."

"Who gets to decide when the time is right?" Abby asked. "Just you? And what is 'right,' anyway? When everything is in perfect order? I think you can forget that, especially with this family."

"Amen to that," Nell said. "To borrow an expression from my late husband, it's time to fish or cut bait, Megan. And I think Jess is right. It makes perfect sense to get married when you're not in the middle of plans for your business. Once you start moving forward with that, you'll have too much on your mind to enjoy your big day."

"Exactly, Mom," Jess said.

Megan knew they all had her best interests at heart. She also knew how much they wanted to see her back with Mick. What she didn't understand was why they couldn't see that no marriage should start off with so much turmoil surrounding it. It was difficult enough to make a marriage work when all the stars were aligned propitiously at the outset.

Jess sighed deeply. "She's still not buying it," she said when Megan said nothing.

"I'm sorry, but I can't," Megan said.

"Okay, what's the biggest hurdle?" Bree asked. "Forget about Connor and Heather. That's his mess to resolve. Is it your relationship with Connor that's the biggest roadblock to a wedding, or is it this thing about the loan?"

"They're both important," Megan said.

"Then I'll talk to Connor and straighten him out," Jess said with blithe certainty that she could handle her brother.

"And I'll work out other financing arrangements," Abby said just as decisively. "Just give me a copy of your business plan. I'll take it from there."

Bree beamed at Megan. "That ought to do it. Anything else?"

Megan gave them a wry look. They made it sound so simple, which just proved how naive they all were. "Come back to me when you've resolved those two problems, and we'll talk," she challenged.

Her daughters stood up. "Shall we meet back here tomorrow?" Jess asked.

"Works for me," Bree said.

"I'm supposed to be in Baltimore, but I'll make it work," Abby chimed in. "Getting this resolved is too important for me to miss it."

Megan listened as they left, still chattering excitedly.

"You do know they're going to pull this off, don't

you?" Nell said, regarding her with amusement. "Then what will you do? Do you have any more excuses up your sleeve?"

"If they accomplish the impossible, especially by tomorrow, then I'll get fitted for a wedding dress," she promised.

But she didn't think there was a snowball's chance in hell it would be an issue.

11

Mick slipped out to the porch after dinner to smoke his pipe and make a few calls. He was dying to know what had gone on around here this afternoon when the girls had come over to cheer Megan up. She'd been surprisingly tight-lipped over dinner, even when he'd asked her point-blank how the visit had gone.

He'd planned to start with Jess, who was usually all too eager to share her opinions with him. As soon as he dialed, though, he heard the sound of a ringing phone nearby. When Jess answered, he looked around.

"Where the devil are you?" he asked.

"In your driveway," she responded. "Where are you?"

"On the porch."

"Ah! I can smell your pipe tobacco from here." She turned the corner of the house and grinned at him. "Do Mom and Gran know you're out here sneaking a smoke?"

"It's a pipe, and those two don't tell me what to do," he grumbled. "What are you doing over here for the second time today? Did you and your mother make plans to get together again to talk about the wedding?"

"Afraid not," she said. "I am on a prewedding mission, though. I'm supposed to whip Connor into line. Is he here? I didn't see his car."

"It's probably parked around back. He's upstairs with his son," Mick said. "What exactly are you hoping to accomplish?"

"Mom agreed—well, pretty much, anyway—that she'd go through with the wedding if we could fix her relationship with Connor and get the financing for the gallery in order. Abby's working on the financing tonight. I'm working on Connor."

He regarded her with amusement. "I like the plan. I don't hold out a lot of hope for your part in it, though. Connor's not listening to anybody these days."

"He'll listen to me," Jess said confidently. "I was a lot more damaged by Mom's leaving than he ever was, and I've forgiven her." She shrugged. "Mostly, anyway. He can do the same, or at least go through the motions till we get this wedding done. I've turned down three other events for New Year's Eve because you booked the inn. I do not intend to lose business because Connor's stubborn."

Mick shook his head. "Good luck with that," he said. "Let me know how it turns out. Something tells me you'll be back down here with your tail between your legs in less than five minutes."

"Oh, ye of little faith," Jess retorted. "I know too many of his secrets for him to toss me out without listening to what I have to say."

Mick stared at her. "You're going to blackmail your brother?"

"If necessary," she said happily. "It wouldn't be the first time. I discovered a long time ago that being a nosy little sister definitely has its perks."

Mick shook his head and let her go just as his cell phone rang.

"It's me, Dad," Abby said. "Can you talk?"

"Ever known me not to?" he asked.

"I mean is Mom around?"

"No, she's inside helping Gram clean up after dinner."

"Ah, you've left them to their women's work," Abby said dryly. "Why am I not surprised?"

"Did you call just to give me grief?"

"No, I called because I need money for Mom's gallery."

"She doesn't want my money," Mick reminded Abby.

"She's not going to know it's yours. I'm putting together an investor group, which will buy shares. You'll have the most, Trace and I will have some, and the others will each take a few. Even Gram is chipping in. All Mom will know is that she has backing for the gallery."

"Do you honestly think you can pull this off?" Mick asked skeptically. "If you come back to her in twenty-four hours with financing, she's bound to wonder where you found it so fast."

"I found it so fast because I spend my life putting together deals for people looking for solid investments," Abby said. "I am very good at my job. I don't think she'll question that, especially if I'm as convincing as I intend to be."

Mick chuckled at the devious plan. He couldn't have dreamed up a better one himself. "Count me in. Just give me an amount and I'll have the check ready whenever you want it."

"I'm thinking if I open an account and deposit all the checks first thing in the morning and hand her the checkbook, she'll find it much more difficult to say no."

"You really are a chip off the old block, aren't you?" he said, pleased. "I wish I'd come up with this scheme myself."

"You were too intent on a straightforward approach," Abby said. "I've included a payment plan so she'll be able to buy out the initial investors over time, which will make her very happy. This is strictly business, albeit with family."

"You know she's going to kill you if she figures out that part," Mick said.

"I'm willing to take my chances to make this wedding happen," Abby said, sounding determined.

"Why don't I meet you at the bank first thing in the morning?" Mick suggested.

"We're not doing this here," Abby said. "I'm using a bank in Baltimore. It'll look more legitimate that way. Besides, why should Lawrence get one dime of a return on this? I intend to laugh in his face myself when Mom's gallery is a huge success."

"Invite me along for that," Mick said. "Does Trace mind that you're out to show up his father?"

"Are you kidding me? He was the one who insisted on the Baltimore bank."

"I do like that man of yours," Mick said approvingly.

"I'll tell him you said so," Abby said. "Let me go, Dad. If you can, drop off that check over here first thing in the morning, okay?"

"I can bring it over now, if you like."

"No, I'm about to have a rare hour of quiet time with my husband. Morning's soon enough. Love you."

"Love you, too."

Mick hung up the phone, feeling considerably more optimistic. When he realized that Connor hadn't yet tossed Jess out on her ear, he felt even better. Maybe these sneaky kids of his were going to accomplish what he hadn't been able to on his own and get Megan down the aisle on time, after all. Of course, he did have an ace of his own up his sleeve, and tonight he intended to play that.

Megan was exhausted. The day's emotional ups and downs had taken a toll. All she wanted to do was soak in a relaxing bubble bath, crawl between the sheets of her very comfortable bed and fall asleep in Mick's arms.

At the top of the stairs when she heard Jess and Connor arguing in hushed tones, she tuned it out and went into the room she'd always shared with Mick. When she'd first started coming back to town for visits, Mick had insisted she stay in here while he moved into a guest room down the hall. Lately, though, they'd been sharing the bed they'd bought together right after their honeymoon all those years ago. They'd made a lot of memories—and five children—in this bed.

She grabbed a clean negligee out of a drawer, then went into the bathroom and filled the tub with bubbles and warm water. She lit a couple of candles, then settled in for a good soak. In a matter of seconds her eyes drifted shut.

She was awakened by Mick's touch. He was kneeling beside the tub, a familiar glint in his eyes and a smile on his lips.

"It's a wonder you didn't drown yourself," he said, his fingers skimming down her arm and sending delicious waves of pleasure through her.

"I knew I was safe. I knew you'd be along soon," she said. "Help me up?"

As she rose, the few remaining bubbles slid provocatively down her naked body. Mick couldn't seem to tear his gaze away, but to her surprise, he was backing up instead of taking her in his arms as he had so many other nights.

"Mick?"

"Now that you're out of the tub, I have to go," he said, his voice thick with unmistakable desire.

"Go where?"

"To the guest room."

"What?"

"I told you I wasn't sleeping with you or doing anything intimate with you until after the wedding," he said, even though it seemed to take him a great deal of effort to choke the words out.

Megan recalled the seemingly idle threat, but stared at him in disbelief. "You can't be serious."

"I am," he said, nodding hard. "Very serious."

She took a step toward him, still not wearing a thing. Water beaded on her skin. "You're honestly going to walk out on me now?" she asked.

"I am," he said stoically. "Sometimes we have to sacrifice for the greater good."

"You sound more like a politician than the man I love. What greater good are you talking about?"

"Our future," he said.

Megan sighed. So, she thought, he was going through with his ridiculous scheme to withhold sex until after they married. Didn't he remember that she'd lived without his arms around her for years? She could do it for a few more weeks, or even months, if need be.

She deliberately shrugged as if his decision didn't matter to her. "Suit yourself," she said, reaching for a towel and wrapping it tightly around her body.

In the mirror, she saw his gaze narrow. She hid a grin at the precise moment when he realized she wasn't going to take the bait.

"Good night, Mick," she said cheerfully. "Feel free to take your own pillow, if you like. The ones in the guest room are harder than you prefer. If you're banishing yourself, you might as well be comfortable, since it could be a long time before you're welcome back in here."

He froze in the doorway. "What the devil is that supposed to mean?"

"That if you want to make this some kind of challenge, I can hold out just as long as you can. Seems a little crazy to me, but I'm up for it if you are."

She walked past him into the bedroom and locked the door behind her, which left him to exit into the hallway or to stand there pounding on the door and risk being overheard by Connor, Jess and even his mother. She knew he wouldn't risk that kind of humiliation.

"Good night, Mick," she said, then used a remote to flip off the lights, including those in the bathroom.

She heard his muttered curse, then the hallway door opened and closed with a bang. Sitting on the side of the bed, she laughed. Check and checkmate! Even when he was behaving like an idiot, she had more fun with Mick O'Brien than she'd ever had with any other man, which was one reason she knew without a doubt that this was where she belonged. The only thing in doubt was the timetable.

Megan was in the kitchen with her second cup of tea in the morning when Connor appeared, his son in his arms.

"Shouldn't you have left for work by now?" she asked.

"I should have, but the baby was fussy. I think he might be catching a cold. Was he outside yesterday?"

"Your father and I took him into town," Megan admitted, reaching out to put her hand on the baby's forehead. "He is a little warm. Did you take his temperature?"

"Of course I did," Connor replied irritably. "It's a little high, but nothing to worry about at this point. What were you and Dad thinking taking him out?"

Megan regarded him with exasperation. "We were thinking he'd enjoy the outing. He was dressed warmly enough. I saw to that."

"But this time of year, everyone and their brother is wandering around with cold and flu symptoms."

"Are you honestly suggesting that you and Heather never took him anywhere?"

Connor sighed as he tried to put the baby into his high chair. "Of course not. I just had a busy day at work today. Having to cancel all those meetings annoyed me, so I'm taking it out on you."

"You don't have to stay here," Megan reminded him. "I'm here to look after the baby. Between your grandmother and me, we have more than enough experience dealing with a little cold, if that's what he has."

"What if it's more serious?" Connor asked. "You don't know his doctor."

"Couldn't you give us the name?" she asked reasonably. "And if he wants us to bring him in, we could probably even manage that."

Connor looked torn. "You're right. I know you are. I just hate to leave him. He looks so miserable."

"And he could be perfectly fine in an hour, and you'll have wasted the whole day," Megan argued. "Go to work. I promise I'll call you if he seems even a tiny bit worse."

"I'll feel like such an awful dad if I go," Connor said.

"Sweetheart, you will not be the first parent to go to work when there's a sick child at home. You're leaving him with family, not abandoning him."

"Are you sure it's okay?"

"Absolutely," she said.

He was halfway to the door when he turned back. "Thanks, Mom. I owe you."

"You don't owe me anything," she assured him.

He came back anyway and pressed a kiss to her

forehead. "At the least, I owe you an apology for being so blasted stubborn," he insisted.

He left before she could respond to his startling words. Was it possible that Jess had gotten through to him, after all? Megan wouldn't have given two cents for the chances that he would listen to anyone, but it certainly seemed as if something had changed overnight.

Still, it was just one step on the long road to real reconciliation.

Mick had been growling at anyone who crossed his path all morning. He hadn't expected Megan to turn the tables on him the night before. The infuriating woman had stood right there as naked as the day she was born, clearly trying to seduce him, then walked away as if it were all a huge joke when he'd turned her down. He hadn't slept a wink all night because of it.

"Don't you look cheery," Abby noted when he arrived at her place to deliver the promised check. "Need some coffee to put you in a better mood?"

"I've had coffee," he said. "It didn't help. I doubt a stiff drink would help."

Abby chuckled. "What's Mom done now?"

"You don't want to know," he said, aware that to tell the story would probably reflect worse on him than it would on Megan. "Where are the twins?"

"Trace just took them to school. I'm leaving for Baltimore in a few minutes." She studied him intently. "Unless you need to talk."

"Nothing to say. I hope this plan of yours works. I need to drive over and check on my Habitat for Humanity sites this morning. You can reach me on my cell if you need me."

"Okay," she said, regarding him with a puzzled expression. "Did you and Mom have a fight?"

"No. Now drop it. We both have places to go."

Still feeling out of sorts, he went back to his car. He started to head toward one of his project sites, but instead took a turn and drove toward Annapolis instead. He was as surprised as his brother was when he turned up at Thomas's office.

"Mick!" Thomas said, standing up with a smile on his face. "I didn't expect to see you today. Is there a problem of some kind? Is Ma okay?"

"Ma's fine," Mick said, looking around at the cramped office. Every surface was covered with stacks of what looked like reports of some kind. He'd expected something fancier for the head of an organization dedicated to protecting the Chesapeake Bay. Clearly they weren't spending their funding on accessories or even furniture, if the scarred desk and chairs in here were any indication. He had to admit he was impressed with his brother's determination to put every cent into the project's goals.

"You have any coffee?" he asked eventually.

"Sure," Thomas said. "Move that pile of papers." He pointed to a stack beside his desk. "I think there's a chair under there. I'll be right back with the coffee."

Mick nodded, located the chair and sat, wondering what the hell had brought him here this morning. It had been an instinctive decision. There'd been a time long ago when he'd respected his younger brother's opinion. And, truth be told, there wasn't anyone he knew who understood more about women and how their minds worked. Somehow Thomas was still friends with the two women he'd married and divorced.

When Thomas came back with two cups of coffee, he handed one to Mick. "So, what brings you by? You've never set foot in here before."

"Too stubborn," Mick said candidly. He shrugged.

"Doesn't mean I haven't been curious, especially since Kevin came to work with you."

"And that's what brought you here today? Curiosity?"

Mick regarded his brother warily. "Can I trust you not to make too much of this?"

"Since I have no idea what you're talking about, it's hard to say, but anything you want to talk about I can keep to myself, if that's what you're really asking."

Mick nodded. "Okay, then, here it is. I need some advice."

"About?"

Mick hesitated, knowing that once he said what was on his mind, he was in danger of having his brother laugh his fool head off. Still, he was here. "Women," he said eventually.

Thomas, blast him, laughed, just as Mick had feared he might. Then he sobered and regarded Mick with genuine sympathy. "Megan's tied you in knots, has she?"

Mick gave him a rueful look. "Something like that. I want to get this show on the road and marry her, but she keeps coming up with excuses."

"Are they legitimate excuses?"

"She'd say so."

"But you disagree?"

"I'm just worried that even if these things get resolved, she'll find more reasons why the timing isn't right."

"Mick, surely you're not worried that the woman doesn't love you," he said, looking incredulous. "That much is plain to anyone. Megan was crazy in love with you when the two of you married years ago. She was just as deeply in love when she walked out. As far as I can see, that hasn't changed. You just have to be patient. I know that's not your best virtue, but I think you have to find some way to give her whatever time she needs."

"I just don't understand why, if she loves me so much, this has to be so complicated."

"It just is, at least for her. She's worth waiting for, don't you think?"

"I've been waiting all these years, haven't I?" Mick said impatiently.

"Then what's a few more weeks or months?"

"I'm just afraid it'll turn into years," he admitted.

"And what if it does?" Thomas asked reasonably. "The difference will only be that she doesn't have your ring on her finger." His gaze narrowed. "Or do you think she might walk away again?"

"I don't know," Mick admitted.

"If there's one thing *I* know, Mick, it's that there are no guarantees in life. She could walk away even if you get that ring on her finger. She did before. What counts is how happy you can make her while she's there. You do that well enough, there's no question she'll stick around. And in the end, isn't that what really matters?"

"Maybe you can take things as they come, the way you've just implied, but I want the ring," Mick said wistfully. "I want the commitment. I guess I'm more old-fashioned than I ever realized. I always thought Jeff was the stodgy one among us."

Thomas laughed. "He is. You just like to know when something is yours. Sadly, though, people aren't like possessions. They stay as long as they want to. Sometimes that's forever. Sometimes not."

A sad look passed across Thomas's face. Mick caught it and regarded him with surprise. "You still miss them, don't you?"

"Miss who?" Thomas said evasively, a flush on his cheeks.

"Both of them. Your wives."

Thomas didn't bother trying to deny it. "I suppose I do. I liked being married. I loved both of them. I just couldn't be the kind of husband either of them needed. This isn't a nine-to-five job. I'm passionate about what I do, and I feel this tremendous sense of urgency to get the job done and get it done right."

"I can relate to that," Mick said. "We're quite a pair, aren't we? A couple of middle-aged men still trying to get it right when it comes to women."

"But you've got the brass ring within reach," Thomas said. "Grab it and hold on." He gave him a surprisingly wise look. "But not so tightly that she doesn't have the freedom she needs. Remember that, Mick. Megan's not a possession. She's a partner."

"I've figured out that much." He studied his younger brother. "What about you? When are you going to find the right woman?"

"I'm not looking at the moment," Thomas said. "Things here are pretty demanding, and I've learned my lesson. No woman likes being left on the back burner while I'm here trying to save one little corner of the world."

"What you need is a partner, just like you said a minute ago. You need someone who'll care about this as much as you do."

"You find a woman out there like that, send her to me," Thomas said.

"I know you're joking, but I've been known to do some successful matchmaking in my time," Mick said. "And I owe you for listening today and not laughing in my face. Well, except for that once, anyway."

"We're brothers," Thomas said simply. "And wouldn't it make Ma happy if she could see us now?"

Mick nodded. "I believe I'll tell her I stopped by. It will make her day." He started for the door. "You'll be with us on Christmas?"

"Of course," Thomas said, then grinned. "If it's as exciting as Thanksgiving, it should be quite a day."

"Bite your tongue," Mick said. "I'm hoping for peace and quiet."

"At an O'Brien gathering? Not likely."

Mick sighed. "I can always dream, can't I? At least maybe you and I can keep the fussing to a minimum."

"There's always a chance," Thomas agreed.

As Mick drove back to the first of his job sites, he felt a thousand times better. It wasn't as if anything in his life were resolved, but it was surprisingly comforting to have his brother on his side at least for now. He'd missed that unconditional backup more than he'd realized.

12

Megan was rocking the baby, who'd finally fallen into a restless sleep, when the portable phone in her pocket rang. She grabbed it quickly, hoping it wouldn't wake little Mick. Though he was much improved over the day before when they'd thought he was coming down with a cold, he was still fussier than usual.

"Hello," she said in a whisper.

"Who is this?" a soft, feminine voice asked tentatively.

"It's Megan O'Brien," Megan said at once, knowing intuitively who was on the other end of the line. "Heather, is it you?"

Silence greeted the question.

"Heather?"

"I just need to know how my baby is," she said, which was answer enough. "Is he with you, or did Connor come for him?"

"I have him in my arms right now," Megan told her. "He just fell asleep."

"Then Connor didn't come," she said, sounding disappointed.

"Of course he did," Megan assured her. "He's been staying here and commuting to Baltimore. Where are you, Heather? He's been trying everywhere to reach you."

"I don't think I can talk to him right now," she said staunchly. "I need to figure out some things, and I can't do that when I'm around Connor. He's always been able to talk me into doing whatever he wants, even when I know it's wrong. I have to start thinking about what *I* want, and what my baby needs."

"I understand why you might need some space from Connor right now," Megan said. "But what about the baby? Don't you want to see him?"

"Desperately," Heather said, her voice choked.

"Then come here," Megan pleaded. "Connor won't be back until this evening. You could spend a couple of hours with little Mick and be gone before he gets home, if that's what you really want. Or you could stay and explain how you're feeling. Connor might understand, you know."

"I can't take the chance," Heather said. She hesitated, then said, "I know it's a lot to ask, but could you bring the baby to see me? I'm not that far away."

Megan knew Connor would probably disapprove, but she also understood Heather's need to see her child. And someone needed to see the baby's mother in person and make sure she was okay. If Heather trusted her, then Megan had no choice but to go.

"Tell me where you are," she said decisively.

Heather gave her an address for a hotel in a small town less than twenty-five miles away.

"I'll be there in an hour, perhaps less," Megan promised.

"Thank you so much," Heather said, clearly relieved. "This means the world to me."

"Believe me, I understand that," Megan said, thinking of what it would have meant to her to have someone bring her children for a visit after she'd moved away. She could never wish that kind of heart-wrenching loneliness and regret on another mother.

Nell came home from church just as Megan was carrying the baby out to the car. She regarded them with surprise.

"Where are you two off to?" she asked Megan.

"Heather called," she admitted. "I'm taking the baby to her for a visit."

Nell regarded her with dismay. "Have you spoken to Connor? Does he know about this?"

Megan shook her head. "I'll tell him tonight."

"He's going to be furious," Nell predicted. "The two of you will wind up right back where you started. Are you sure you want to take that chance?"

"I don't think I have a choice," Megan said, not denying the potential consequences. "Heather needs to see her son. No one can understand that better than I."

Nell nodded. "I can't deny that, and I certainly understand that poor girl's desire to see her baby. Will you be gone long?"

"A few hours at most. I should be back here long before Connor gets home from work."

"Drive safely, then. See if you can persuade that

young woman to come back here with you. She
should be here, trying to work things out with Connor."

"I've already tried, but she seems dead set against
it for the moment. I'll keep trying, though."

The drive, through winding country roads, didn't
take long at all. In less than forty minutes, she was
pulling into a parking spot by the small hotel. She'd
barely cut the engine when she spotted Heather running across the parking lot. Weeping openly, she
flung open the back door and gathered her son into
her arms before Megan could even emerge from behind the wheel. Megan watched the reunion with
tears in her eyes.

"Can you stay?" Heather asked, her expression
plaintive. "Please. There's a little coffee shop inside."

"Of course we'll stay," Megan said, compassion
welling up for the young woman.

Inside the tiny, but spotless coffee shop, they ordered coffee, though Heather never touched hers. She
couldn't seem to stop caressing her baby's cheek,
smoothing his hair and tickling his tummy. His giggles were the happiest sounds Megan had heard him
make in days. The deep bond between mother and

child was obvious. The bond was there with Connor, too, of course, but this was something special to see.

"Heather, I know a bit about what's been going on between you and Connor. Won't you reconsider and come back to Chesapeake Shores with me? I just know the two of you can work things out. He loves you."

"Not enough," Heather said sadly. "I've finally had to accept that."

"I think you're wrong. I do think he loves you enough, and if you're just a little more patient, I think he'll change his mind about getting married."

"It's not even about that," Heather said. "At least not entirely. It's the kind of work he does, his whole cynical outlook on life. I'm an optimistic person. I believe in love. How can I possibly be with someone who helps people break up their marriages because that's what he expects to happen to every couple? How could I be with someone who doesn't think love can last a lifetime?"

"You know that his father and I set a bad example," Megan said. "It would be hard for anyone to look beyond that."

"Most of your children have," Heather said. "He's told me all about Kevin's marriage and Abby's and

Bree's reunions with their childhood sweethearts. How can he see them and not believe that anything's possible?"

"I think a part of him desperately wants to believe, but it's hard for him to let go of his memories of his parents' divorce, especially with the line of law he's in reinforcing the cynicism day in and day out."

"Well, I don't want to live with all that negativity," Heather said. "And I hate the way he's been treating you, when you've been trying so hard to make amends. It's just wrong. I think that was the last straw, when he decided to stand in the way of you marrying his father."

Megan smiled at her passionate defense. "You do realize that's my battle to fight, not yours," she said gently. "Not that I don't appreciate the support, but the last thing I want to do is become one more obstacle between the two of you."

Heather gave her a rueful look. "Trust me, you're just one thing on a long list."

"Okay, then, let me ask you something else. If you believe in love as you say you do and you love my son so deeply, why don't you trust that you and Connor can overcome all these obstacles, however many there are?"

Heather lifted her gaze from the baby. "Because I can't do it alone, and Connor won't even try."

"I think he might, but you have to give him that chance. You've made your point. Can't you at least talk to him? Nothing can ever be resolved if there's no communication. I sometimes wonder if Mick and I would have divorced years ago, if I'd made it clear to him how I was feeling, and he'd really had the chance to change his ways."

"It's too soon for me to see Connor," Heather insisted, sounding just as stubborn as any O'Brien ever had. "I will, though. I promise." She held Megan's gaze. "Please don't tell him where I am. Not yet."

"I have to tell him I brought the baby to see you," Megan said.

"That's okay. I understand. Just don't tell him I'm here. I need more time. I need to get stronger, feel more sure of myself."

Megan regarded her with regret. "I can give you that much," Megan promised her. "But, sweetie, don't drag this out. Take it from me, it will only get harder to swallow your pride and reach out."

Heather nodded. "I do know that." She gave Megan a pleading look. "Will you come again? Please."

Megan hesitated, then nodded. "Anytime you want

me to." At least it would keep the lines of communication open and she would know how to reach Heather. Someone needed to have that information, and it had been entrusted to her.

And yet she knew it could be a double-edged sword, because as Nell had worried earlier, Connor might very well not forgive her, not for coming here today and not for keeping Heather's location a secret.

When Mick showed up at Harbor Lights the afternoon before the town's annual boat parade, he anticipated finding Kevin struggling to decorate the boat he'd donated to Thomas's research team. He hadn't expected to find Connor untangling a string of lights, not after the way Kevin had complained about having to do all of the work alone. He could have sworn Connor had gone off to work today, same as usual, without exchanging more than a terse word or two with either of his parents.

Mick stood on the dock, his expression uneasy. "Where's your brother?"

Connor's scowl was every bit as deep as Mick's probably was. "He went to get coffee. He claimed the stove in the galley's not working." He regarded

Mick with suspicion. "I assume he knew you were coming by."

"He insisted on it," Mick said. "You?"

"Same thing."

"Your brother's a sneaky son of a gun," Mick said, debating whether to stay or go.

"Takes one to know one," Connor replied. "As long as you're here, you might as well make yourself useful. There are dozens of strands of lights, and not a one of them hasn't been twisted into knots."

Mick hesitated, then jumped on board. He doubted he and Connor were likely to resolve anything, but maybe they could at least find a way to start talking to each other again, even if it was all about Christmas lights. He looked at the mess that had been stored in a couple of oversize boxes.

"Why the devil doesn't anyone put these things away neatly?" he groused as he tried to extract a single strand and came away with what seemed to be miles of cord.

"I think they do," Connor said, his brow furrowed as he worked on a tangled mess. "I'm pretty sure Christmas lights have some magical way of twisting into knots after they're packed. You've been complaining about the same thing at home ever since

I was a kid and I know we always put those lights away in tidy rows, carefully separated from each other. Mom insisted on it in a futile attempt to keep you from making the same complaint every year."

"Kevin must have learned his packing system from her, then, because it sure doesn't work," Mick said as he managed to separate one strand of lights from the rest. He plugged it in to test it, found several bulbs burned out and replaced those, then set it aside.

They worked in silence for a while, then Mick said, "You planning to come back to the house when you're finished here?"

Connor glanced his way, his expression puzzled. "Of course. I've been there every day since Heather dropped off my son. Why would today be any different?"

Mick flushed guiltily. He'd heard from his mother about Megan's trip to see Heather this afternoon. If Connor got back to the house before they did, there'd be hell to pay. "Just asking," he said, resolving to call Megan's cell phone the first chance he had to warn her that Connor had come home early from Baltimore, assuming he'd ever gone to work at all.

Connor's gaze narrowed with suspicion. "What's

going on back at the house that you don't want me to know about?"

Mick shrugged. "No idea what you mean."

"Dad, I've cross-examined pathological liars and seen through it. You're a lot easier to read. What's going on?"

Mick settled for a half-truth. "Your mother took the baby out to visit someone this afternoon. I didn't want you turning up there and pitching a fit about it the way you did when we took him into town the other day."

"I overreacted," Connor admitted. "I thought he was coming down with something and was looking for someone to blame. It always scares me when he gets sick. He's so little and helpless and he can't say what's wrong. I apologized to Mom about that."

They fell silent as they worked on the lights. Eventually Mick said, "You and I haven't talked much since all of this happened. Just so you know, I am glad you're at home looking after your boy. The two of you belong here with us."

Connor looked surprised, then nodded. "Thanks, Dad. I am sorry little Mick got dumped in your lap."

"What I'm sorry about is that you didn't see fit to tell any of us about him in the first place," Mick said. "What were you thinking, Connor? An O'Brien is supposed to do the right thing by the mother of his child."

Connor immediately bristled. "The right thing being to get married, I suppose."

"That would be a fine start," Mick agreed, even though he knew they were heading straight into dangerous territory.

"You know how I feel about that, Dad. Eventually marriage always leads to heartache. I see a steady stream of clients whose lives are filled with regrets over taking that step."

"And you have a whole family to look to who've found happiness being married to people they love," Mick replied.

Connor looked unconvinced. "Abby, Bree and Kevin?" he scoffed. "They haven't been married long enough to be good examples. Now, you and Mom? You set the bar. Close to twenty years together and five kids, and it still fell apart."

"Not because we didn't love each other," Mick insisted. "Because I made mistakes."

"So did Mom. Have you forgotten the man she was seeing while you were out of town?"

"I haven't forgotten it, but I understand it and I've

forgiven her. Since you and your brother talk, you must know there was no affair to forgive. I've told him that repeatedly."

"What about the fact that she turned to another man in the first place? Isn't that as bad as having an affair?"

Truthfully, it had put a huge dent in Mick's ego and his heart. In the end, though, his heart had weathered it, and his ego had realized that what happened was in many ways his own fault. Megan had sought attention from someone else because he wasn't around. She'd tried to tell him a thousand different ways how she was feeling, but he'd been too busy to really listen.

"Son, there are mistakes in all marriages. The test is how you handle them. Maybe if I'd understood then what I do now about why Megan had been seeing someone else, I could have fixed things before she took that final step and left me."

He met Connor's gaze and saw that his son didn't really buy anything he was saying. "Look, don't pattern your life or your relationships on mine. That's a sure way to wind up losing what you really want." He gave Connor a hard look. "You do want Heather and your son in your life, don't you?"

"Heather understood the rules from the moment we started dating," Connor said defensively, avoiding the question. "She knew all along how I felt about marriage. It's nothing but a piece of paper with no more power to control someone's behavior than a contract that someone doesn't want to honor. The only difference is it doesn't have all the loopholes spelled out in the fine print."

Connor's cynicism was deeply disturbing, especially since Mick felt at least partially responsible for it. Whatever lessons he and Megan had taught him by divorcing had been reinforced by his chosen career.

He gave Connor a knowing look. "Think about this a minute and then tell me the truth. Are you feeling any less pain today over Heather's leaving than you would if the two of you had been married?"

Connor remained silent too long, which was answer enough.

"I thought so," Mick said. "It's not the piece of paper that's important, son. It's what's in your heart. Those divorce papers I signed didn't change anything, either. No matter how hurt and angry I was, I knew I'd love your mother till the day I died. Now I have a chance to have her back in my life, and I'm not going to blow it." He gave Connor a pointed look. "I won't let anyone else blow this chance for us, either."

Connor frowned at the warning, but said nothing.

Mick persisted. "I know your sister got on your case about this the other night. Did she get through to you?"

"She tried," Connor admitted. "I said I'd try to keep a more open mind."

Mick sighed. It was probably the best he could hope for.

Kevin returned just then with a take-out tray of large coffees and a bag filled with still-warm crois-sants from Sally's. He eyed the two of them hope-fully.

"Looks as if no blood's been shed," he commented as he hopped easily on board, then handed out the coffee and pastries. "I was a little concerned I'd come back and find a body stowed belowdeck."

"Not until we get these dang lights untangled," Mick said. "And you're selling us short. We're both smart enough not to leave a body on board. Either one of us would have taken the boat out to sea and dumped the body overboard."

Connor chuckled for the first time since Mick's

arrival. "Nice to know just how devious your mind is, Dad."

"He's probably been plotting a way to get even with Uncle Thomas for years," Kevin guessed. "I'll have to warn him about going out to sea with Dad."

"I'm not going to do away with your uncle," Mick retorted indignantly, wondering what his sons would think if he admitted to having a heart-to-heart with Thomas just days ago. "If I were, I wouldn't have waited all these years to do it. You weren't even a glimmer in my eye when he betrayed me. I've had plenty of time to get even, if I were going to."

"No, instead he's just frozen him out," Connor said. "That's so much better. Up until today, I figured that was going to be my fate, too."

"Which is precisely why I interceded," Kevin said. "This kind of nonsense in our family has gone on long enough. Have the two of you settled anything?"

Mick shrugged. "Connor's the one who's being stubborn."

Connor stared at him incredulously. "Pot calling the kettle black."

Kevin laughed. "I think we can agree, this family

is full of stubborn men. A few mule-headed women, too, for that matter. The point is, we are a family. Let's not forget that."

"Fair enough," Mick agreed, regarding Connor hopefully. "Son?"

"I can bury the hatchet," Connor said eventually. "Since my son seems to be here for the foreseeable future, I don't really have a choice."

"You could take him back to Baltimore, then find his mother and marry her," Mick suggested.

Connor scowled at the suggestion. "Maybe we should make a pact," Connor said. "You stay out of my relationship and I'll try to stay out of yours."

Mick laughed at the thought of any O'Brien minding his own business for long. "It's a fool's pact, but why not?"

Kevin beamed at them. "Now kiss and make up," he ordered, his voice laced with humor.

"Careful, bro, or you'll be the one who's tossed overboard," Connor warned.

"At least he'll go knowing the two of us are co-operating on something," Mick added. He held up a hand and Connor slapped it. It was a rare moment of solidarity with his son and, as ridiculous as it was, it gave him hope.

* * *

The lighted boat parade, first launched two years after Chesapeake Shores had been fully developed, was one of Megan's favorite community events. Back then, she and Mick hadn't had a boat, but many in the community had them, everything from rowboats and kayaks to fancy speedboats and huge yachts.

The competition among the town's home owners to outdo each other with outdoor holiday decorations had extended to their boats. Standing onshore to watch as these lighted vessels floated by on the bay had always brought out the holiday spirit in her. She and Mick would bundle up the kids and sit in the yard with the smallest ones in their laps as the boats paraded upstream and then back down.

When the kids were older, they'd gone down to the marina after the parade. Harbor Lights always hosted a party that offered gallons of hot chocolate for the kids and stiffer drinks for the adults. A wide variety of hors d'oeuvres was available for purchase from various restaurants to benefit the town's Christmas fund to buy toys for needy families in the region. Next to the tree-lighting ceremony, it was Chesapeake Shores' most popular holiday event.

For the second time, Kevin had entered his research boat in the parade. Megan could hardly wait to see it. Last year Phillip's gallery had had an opening on the same night, and she hadn't been able to get away from New York to come home for the boat parade.

"Daddy Kevin's is the best boat in the whole parade," Henry assured her excitedly as the family gathered at the shoreline waiting for the parade to start. "Next year me and Davy get to ride on it. Mom said it was too cold tonight for us to be on the water."

"And she was absolutely right," Megan told him, securing a wool scarf more tightly around his neck. "It must be below freezing out here." She checked to see that Davy was bundled up warmly enough, then saw that Abby was doing the same with Carrie and Caitlyn.

"I swear next year I'm going to insist they do this in October," Abby said, shivering despite her fur-lined, hooded parka.

"Which is the obvious time to do a Christmas parade," Trace commented. "Do you think you'll get a lot of support?"

Abby scowled at him. "Okay, you get to deal with the twins when they both come down with colds this week," she said.

Trace grinned. "Hey, I'm the stay-at-home dad. I deal with them whenever they get anything. You don't scare me."

"Nobody's going to get sick," Mick declared, as if it were something he could control. He turned to Nell. "Ma, are you warm enough?"

Before she could reply, Davy yelled, "There he is! There's my dad. He's leading the whole parade 'cause he's the best."

"I don't know why he insisted on having Thomas on board with him," Mick grumbled under his breath.

"Maybe because Kevin's given the boat to your brother's research team, so it's technically not his anymore," Megan suggested, amused. "I'm sure you could have joined them. I know perfectly well he invited you."

"And I'd have been listening to some lecture from Thomas from the time we left the dock until we returned. All the man talks about is how development's ruining the bay."

"Not this development," Megan said. "You built Chesapeake Shores in compliance with his very stringent rules."

Mick grimaced. "And fought with him over every darn thing," he recalled. "What did he do when he lost an argument? He turned me in to the authorities."

"But in the end, you both got what you wanted," Megan reminded him. "You developed a community that's won awards for being environmentally friendly, and Thomas protected these waters from more pollution."

She glanced around. "Where's Connor?"

"He said it was too cold for little Mick," Abby said. "He's up at the house with Bree and Jake. I left Connor with the box of ornaments for the tree we're going to decorate after the parade's over. He's supposed to be tossing out the broken ones and dusting the rest. I still don't know how things can possibly get broken just sitting in a box in the attic most of the year."

Megan looked directly at Mick. "Because some people are careless when they put the boxes away or bring them downstairs," she said pointedly.

Mick rolled his eyes at the familiar complaint. "Well, all I can say is better him than me. He's probably conned Jake into taking over by now."

Megan laughed and linked her arm through Mick's. "You know you wouldn't be happy if you couldn't grumble about the tangled lights and all the boxes of ornaments that have to be hauled downstairs. The year I bought all brand-new ones to avoid aggravating you, you complained that it was a waste of money when the others were perfectly fine."

"Dad is nothing if not inconsistent," Abby said.

"Okay, enough bickering," Nell declared. "You all are missing all the beautiful boats. I believe I like the ones with the multicolored lights the best. That's the way we all decorated years ago. It's only recently that everyone's started using the clear lights for everything."

"I agree with you, Nell," Megan said. "The colored lights are much more festive. They feel old-fashioned, too, like the images you see in storybooks."

"But the clear ones make it look like a fairyland," Carrie argued.

"Who wants to go to a dumb old fairyland?" Davy taunted.

"Princesses do," Caitlyn said with a touch of disdain.

"You're not a princess," Davy told her.

"That's what you think, squirt," Caitlyn retorted. "Careful or I'll use my magical powers to turn you into a frog."

Davy turned tear-filled eyes up to Megan. "She can't do that, can she?"

"No, she most certainly cannot," Megan said,

shooting a warning look at her granddaughter. "Now, who wants hot chocolate?"

She asked in the interest of keeping peace, and a chorus of approving shouts greeted the question.

"Okay, then," she said, ready to herd the little ones up to the house.

"Want me to come with you?" Mick asked.

"I'll go," Abby offered. "You stay out here with Gram."

Megan cast a last, regretful look over her shoulder at the boats still on the water, then led the way back to the house. Though she'd wanted to enjoy the rest of the parade, she had to admit it felt good to be indoors. At least it did until she caught a glimpse of Connor snatching up his son and leaving the kitchen. The angry scowl on his face said he could hardly wait to get away from her. She had a feeling she knew what it was about, too: her decision to take the baby to see Heather. She sighed heavily.

"Ignore him, Mom. He's just being impossible. If he keeps it up, kick him out."

"After I criticized your father for doing exactly that? I don't think so," Megan said. "Having the two of us under this roof is the only way we're going to settle anything."

"But his rudeness is wrong," Abby protested. "He's old enough to know better."

"Oh, sweetie, he knows better," Megan said, resigned to accepting whatever punishment he doled out. "He wants me to suffer the way he did."

"But you have suffered. We all made you pay for leaving. We practically cut you out of our lives back then, no matter how hard you tried to make things right. Now that we're grown, I think we all understand more clearly why you did what you did."

"All of you except Connor. I think he's taking some satisfaction in being the last holdout. He didn't have any power over what happened back then. Now he does. Besides, I don't really think his attitude tonight is about any of that."

Abby regarded her curiously. "Well, I don't care what it's about. It needs to stop. I thought Jess had gotten him to shape up. I guess it's up to me after all."

Megan regarded her with alarm. "No, leave it alone, Abby. I won't have this cause a rift between you two."

"You can't order me not to talk to him," Abby said stubbornly.

Megan smiled at the determined lift of her chin.

"No," she said quietly. "But I can ask you not to, as a favor to me."

Abby gave her a disgruntled look. "Not fair," she accused.

Megan smiled. "No, but effective. Don't worry, sweetie. This will all work out."

"Don't count on it," Connor said, walking back into the kitchen with a scowl on his face. He'd apparently put the baby to bed.

"Connor," Abby protested.

"Don't start on me, sis. Are you aware that our mother has been sneaking off with my child to visit Heather?"

Megan flinched. "I can explain."

"Oh, I'm sure you can," Connor said. "But I don't want to hear it. All I know is that once again, when push came to shove, you chose somebody else over your own family."

"I most certainly did not," Megan protested. "Someone needed to know where Heather is. She seemed to trust me. And she needed to see her son."

"I would have been more than happy to take Mick to see her," Connor said angrily. "You didn't allow me the opportunity."

Megan sighed. "Believe me, I tried to get her to

come here. I tried to convince her to see you. She's not ready. What was I supposed to do—deny her the right to see her baby?"

"Yes," Connor snapped.

"Oh, Connor, you don't mean that," Abby said.

Connor whirled on her. "Do not get in the middle of this, sis, not the way Mom has thrown herself into the middle of my situation with Heather." He gave Megan a weary look. "Count your blessings that you have Heather's trust these days, because you've lost mine." He turned to Abby. "As for that little family investment scheme you put together to finance Mom's business, I hope you all don't lose every red cent."

And then he walked out of the kitchen, leaving Megan feeling totally devastated in too many ways to count. She turned to her daughter.

"Abby, what did he mean? What kind of family investment scheme? I thought you said you put that group together with clients you had at work." She should have known it had come together too easily.

"I did," Abby said defensively, a telltale flush in her cheeks. "Everyone involved has other funds invested with me."

"But your father, you and the others, you're my backers?"

Abby nodded. "Even Gram chipped in."

On some level, Megan couldn't help but be grateful for the support they were all demonstrating, but on another, she felt totally betrayed. "Oh, Abby, how could you?"

"Because it's a solid investment, and I didn't want you to lose the chance to have the business you want."

"No, what you really want is for me to go ahead with marrying your father."

"So what?" Abby said defiantly. "Is it wrong to want to see the two of you happy again?"

Megan regarded her sorrowfully. "Not this way, sweetie. Not this way. I can't accept that money."

"You already have. It's in the bank, in your name."

"I'll never touch a dime of it," Megan told her. If there was no other way to finance the gallery, so be it.

As for Connor and his declaration that she'd lost his trust, she'd have to find some way to live with that, too. She knew that given the same situation, she would betray his trust again if it meant bringing Heather and her baby together.

13

Mick walked into the kitchen on the morning after the boat parade to find the baby bundled up in his snowsuit and Connor carrying all of his son's accumulated paraphernalia out to the car. Mick poured himself a cup of coffee and watched for a couple of minutes. When Connor returned for the third time, Mick closed the kitchen door.

"Sit," he ordered.

Connor's scowl deepened. "I don't have time. I need to get my son out of this house."

"Mind telling me why?" Mick inquired reasonably, though he had his suspicions.

"Because I can't trust Mom not to sneak off with him to visit Heather."

Mick nodded. "I figured as much. Now sit down, and take off the baby's snowsuit before he sweats to death in here."

"I'll just have to put it back on when we leave," Connor argued.

"*If* you leave," Mick corrected.

"Oh, I'm leaving. No question about that," Connor insisted.

"Then another half hour or so won't make a bit of difference, will it?"

Connor heaved a resigned sigh and removed little Mick's heavy jacket and pants, then cradled him in his arms. He regarded Mick with a look that dared him to come to Megan's defense.

"How are you going to manage in Baltimore with a baby?" Mick inquired, clearly catching Connor off guard. "Have you made arrangements for a nanny?"

"No, but I'll find someone," Connor said confidently.

"By Monday morning?"

"I know a couple of sitters who can pitch in," Connor replied, though he looked a little less certain.

"We've used them before and I know they're reliable."

"Teenagers?" Mick asked, hazarding a guess.

"So what?" Connor said defensively. "Like I said, we've used them before."

"Won't they have school during the week?" Mick inquired innocently. "They're not on holiday break yet, are they?"

Connor's belligerence faded as he muttered a curse.

"Exactly," Mick said. "Don't you have a big case going before a judge on Monday?"

"Yes," Connor admitted.

Mick shrugged. "I suppose you can always ask for a postponement, though clients who are ready to get their cases over with usually aren't too happy about delays, am I right?"

Connor frowned at him. "What's your point, Dad?"

"That caring for a child and trying to juggle a demanding career isn't easy. It only works if you have backup. You have that here. You don't have it in Baltimore."

"I don't trust Mom," Connor reiterated.

"So you've said. I think what you're really mad about is that Heather didn't get in touch with you."

"Don't be ridiculous," Connor said, then raked a hand through his hair. "Okay, maybe. Mom doesn't have the right to step in and make decisions about who gets to see my son."

"Who has custody of the boy?" Mick asked.

The question silenced Connor, just as Mick had suspected it might. "I'm guessing from your silence that it's Heather," he concluded.

"Technically."

"Then Megan wasn't in the wrong for taking the baby to see her, was she? In fact, I'm guessing Heather could have stirred up a ruckus if she'd refused."

"That's not the issue," Connor said. "Mom went without saying a word to me."

"Were you here?"

"No, but she knows how to reach me. Come on, Dad, you know that's no excuse for leaving me out of the loop. She didn't want to risk having me say no, which is exactly what I would have said."

"You'd have denied Heather the right to see her son?"

"No, I'd have insisted I be the one to take him to see her."

"But Heather didn't want to see you. She made

that clear," Mick said. "And that's what's stuck in your craw, isn't it?"

Connor sighed. "Yes, dammit. Are you happy now?"

"No, I'm just suggesting you cut your mother some slack for doing what she thought was best for your son and for the woman you claim to love. I'm also asking that you think about the consequences of taking off from here without thinking things through."

"You're just worried that if I go it will be one more reason for Mom to postpone the wedding," Connor said. "I suspect after last night, she's having plenty of second thoughts."

Mick scowled at the triumphant note in Connor's voice. Megan had gone off to bed by the time he'd gotten back from the boat parade. If something else had happened, he wasn't aware of it.

"What are you talking about?" he demanded.

"She knows you all put up the money for her business," Connor said. "She wasn't happy about it."

Mick's gaze narrowed. "And exactly how would she find out about that? I doubt Abby admitted it."

Connor had the grace to look vaguely guilty. "I

might have mentioned it when I was fighting with her about Heather."

"Now, why would you do a fool thing like that? You had to know it would blow the plan sky-high," Mick complained. He stared at Connor in dismay. "Of course, that's it, isn't it? You didn't care about the consequences."

"I was angry."

"Do you have any idea what you've done?" Mick demanded, then waved off the question. "Never mind. I'll figure out some way to fix this. In the meantime, forget about me or your mother. Let's focus on what's best for that boy you're holding. He needs to be right here with family until you and his mother work things out."

Mick could see that Connor wanted to contradict him and walk out the door, but he also trusted that his son would do what was best for his child. As furious as he was about this entire mess, one thing Mick knew for certain was that Connor loved that boy.

"Okay," Connor said finally. "But Mom and I have to come to some kind of understanding about Heather."

Mick nodded. "I'll leave that to you. I will warn you about one thing, though. Your mother identifies with Heather and her need to spend time with her child. She won't turn her back on that."

"Not even if I object?"

"Not even if you poke holes in her tires and try to keep her from driving to wherever Heather's hiding out. She'll find a way."

"She sure wasn't that determined to see her own children after she left," Connor complained.

"Some of that was my doing. I was being just as pigheaded as you are right now, trying to keep all of you away from her. Oh, I said all the right words about sharing custody, but I made it too easy for you to refuse to go for visits. And she's still dealing with regrets because she didn't fight me harder. Even if it costs her a relationship with you, she'll do whatever it takes to assure that Heather is able to see her son."

He gave Connor a sly look. "And there's another way to look at this, you know."

"What's that?"

"Your mother loves you. She's probably the best advocate you could have with Heather right now. If there's a way to bring Heather home, your mother will find it. And with Christmas right around the corner, something tells me she'll be highly motivated."

Connor fell silent, clearly pondering Mick's assessment. "Okay," he said finally and with obvious reluctance. "I won't object to Mom taking the baby to visit with Heather. And I'll apologize for some of the things I said last night, including letting the cat out of the bag about the financing."

"You won't regret it," Mick told him, then stood up, satisfied that he'd accomplished what he'd set out to do here this morning. "Now I have a sudden desire for a big breakfast. Sally's pancakes come to mind. Let's bundle that baby back up and go into town."

"Not me," Connor said. "If I'm not going back to Baltimore, then I need to work on my case."

"You want me to take the baby?"

"No. I'll take him upstairs with me. He'll probably nap long enough for me to get some work done."

Mick nodded. "Okay, then. I think I'll see if I can persuade your mother to come along. She and I haven't had more than a few minutes alone in days. I need to try to smoothe her ruffled feathers about the financing."

Connor looked surprised. "But I thought…" He blushed, then said, "Aren't you two back in your old room?"

"My sleeping arrangements are none of your business," Mick said.

His son's eyes lit up. "You've been banished to the guest room again? Uh-oh. What did you do?"

"I overplayed my hand, if you must know," Mick said. "Which is just one more reason I need to get this wedding back on track. I assume you'll stop being a horse's behind and do your part?"

Connor laughed. "When you put the request so sweetly, how can I possibly refuse? Meantime, though, I can hardly wait to share this news with the rest of the family."

"You do and you're dead," Mick warned.

That only made his son laugh even harder. Which just proved that on any given day, a man could win one battle and still lose the war.

Megan had spent an hour helping Nell arrange dozens of handcrafted items on the tables in the church's parish hall. The annual holiday bazaar was one of the church's biggest fundraising events. In addition to the crafts made by members of the church, there was a huge array of home-baked items, along with holiday-themed games for the children.

With only minutes until the doors opened, a half-dozen women were bustling around in the church kitchen to put the finishing touches on the baked-ham lunch that would be available, along with sweet potatoes, macaroni and cheese, green beans and salad. She'd even caught a glimpse of several bright red cherry and lime-green Jell-O molds, as well. Some people would eat the meal right here, while others would take it home. The church even offered a delivery service for those who couldn't stop by for the traditional meal.

Megan turned and caught Nell muttering under her breath. "What's wrong?"

"Have you ever seen so many crocheted doilies in your life?" Nell asked. "Now, I can admire a bit of crochet work as much as the next person, but who has doilies all over the house these days? Trust me, these are going to be right here at the end of the day."

"Maybe not," Megan argued, though she tended to agree with Nell's assessment. "A lot of people admire the handiwork and they want to support the church. Don't they usually sell out?"

"Only after we've marked them down to some rock-bottom price, which ends up insulting Mamie Davis so badly she swears she'll never make another thing for the bazaar. I swear, though, in the time she spends on all of these, she could make a gorgeous tablecloth that would bring in a fortune."

"Why doesn't someone tell her that?" Megan asked.

Nell gave her a disbelieving look. "Maybe you've forgotten Mamie. I've told her myself for at least ten years now, and she comes right back and reminds me that her doilies always sell out. Somehow she blocks out the part about us practically giving them away."

Megan chuckled. "Well, at least this event gets most of the congregation involved, and the whole town loves it."

She looked up as the first rush of customers came through the door, surprised to see Mick among them.

"What are you doing here?" she asked him, not sure she was prepared to deal with him after what she'd learned last night.

"I came to steal you away to go to breakfast with me," he said, winking at Nell. "You don't mind, do you, Ma?"

"Not up to me," she said.

"I promised your mother I'd be here to help today," Megan said. "Besides, I had breakfast hours ago. Why didn't you?"

"Because I was trying to persuade your son not to take his baby and run off to Baltimore," Mick replied.

"Oh, dear," Nell said. "Megan, run along. You probably need to deal with this."

"It's dealt with," Mick insisted, then seemed to realize he'd just gotten in the way of getting what he wanted. "But we do need to talk about what happened. And I understand Connor blabbed about Abby's investment group. We might as well get your reaction to that out in the open."

Megan was surprised by his candor, but she couldn't deny that she appreciated it. She regarded Nell worriedly. "Are you sure you can spare me?"

"I've been working this bazaar since the first one we had a couple of decades ago. I think I can handle one more. Besides, someone will be here to spell me in an hour."

Megan nodded. "Okay, then, if you're sure." She gave Nell a hug. "Don't forget to push those doilies," she whispered. "Do not bring them home with you. I found at least a hundred in a box the other day. I assume those are from years past."

Nell shrugged. "Somebody had to keep that woman from getting her feelings hurt, even if she is a stubborn old coot."

Megan grabbed her folded coat and purse from under a table and joined Mick.

"What was that about?" he asked.

"Nothing," Megan said. "Did you want to look around before we go? Maybe buy a pie or cake for dinner?"

"Ma will be bringing home anything that's left at the end of the day," he said. "Not that there's much left. Usually it's just Hazel West's apple pie."

Megan regarded him with confusion. "What's wrong with Hazel's apple pie?"

"Nothing if you don't care that her cats are wandering around on the counter while she's making it. Once people found out about that, no one wants to eat it."

Megan shuddered. "Yes, I can see why that might be a turnoff."

The chill in the air outside felt good after being cooped up in the overheated parish hall. She took a deep breath. "It smells like Christmas. Don't you think so?"

Mick gave her an inscrutable look. "What exactly does Christmas smell like?"

Megan struggled to put it into words. "The trees from the tree lot by the church, just a hint of snow even though there's absolutely none in the forecast, the excitement in the air."

He laughed. "You can't smell excitement."

"I can," she insisted. "Ask any kid you know. I'll bet Caitlyn, Carrie, Davy and Henry know exactly what I'm talking about."

"You've always been like this around the holidays, haven't you? You get a little crazy and sentimental."

"Of course I do. I love everything about the season, including the carols that are playing in every store and blasting from the speakers on the town green."

"You don't get sick of hearing 'Joy to the World' and 'White Christmas'?"

"How can I? They're classics. I'm always sorry that we put the CDs away the day after Christmas and I don't hear them for another year."

"But you start hearing them again two seconds after Halloween," Mick argued.

"Are you going to be in one of your bah-humbug moods today?" she asked. "If so, you can go to breakfast on your own. I have shopping I could be doing. We've less than two weeks till Christmas. That would suit me just fine. I'm mad at you, anyway."

Mick held up his hands in a gesture of surrender. "Ho-ho-ho," he said, though without much conviction.

"I suppose that'll do," Megan said, following him

into Sally's, which was bustling with others taking a break from shopping or having a late breakfast, as they were.

After they'd ordered—a full breakfast for Mick, a raspberry croissant for her—Megan looked him in the eye. "First things first. Tell me about Connor."

"I caught him packing up the car with the baby's things this morning. He said he was moving back to Baltimore with him."

"I was afraid of that. He was so angry last night. How'd you talk him out of going?"

"I reminded him of the realities of getting the kind of person he needs to look after his son on short notice. I also persuaded him to look at what happened through your eyes. I think he got it."

"Does he know it will happen again if Heather calls?" Megan asked.

"He seems resigned to that, as well." Mick gave her a plaintive look. "Do you *have* to do that? Even though I've explained, it's only going to annoy him. How are we supposed to get him on our side for the wedding, if the two of you are butting heads over this?"

"I can't go against what I believe, that Heather has a right to see her son."

"I don't think Connor disagrees. In fact, I think the real problem is that he wants to be the one who takes the baby to her."

"Heather objects to that. She's not ready to see Connor. I'm afraid if I go against her wishes and tell Connor where she is, she'll just take off and this time take the baby with her."

"I still think we should be trying to get them back together in the same room, instead of letting this separation continue for who knows how long." His eyes lit up. "Next time she calls, maybe I should come along. I can try to talk some sense into her."

Megan could just envision the ruckus that was likely to ensue. "Mick, you don't have a diplomatic bone in your body."

"Forget diplomacy. This calls for tough love. That baby's future is at stake."

"We are not going to meddle," Megan insisted.

"What do you call what you're doing?" he demanded irritably.

"Keeping the lines of communication open between Heather and Connor's family. I have tried to persuade her to see Connor, but I won't try to bully her into it. Neither will you."

Mick sighed. "Were we this stupid and stubborn when we were young?"

Megan laughed. "Sweetheart, some of us still are. Do I need to remind you that you, Abby and the others all went behind my back and lied to me about that financing?"

"We did it with the best of intentions," he reminded her.

She sighed. "I do know that, and it's the only reason I didn't head straight back to New York first thing this morning."

"Then you'll accept the loan?"

She leveled a look into his eyes. "I didn't say that."

"But—"

"Leave it alone, Mick."

"Yes, ma'am," he said, but he didn't look one bit happy about it.

Despite her determined stance when it came to taking the baby to see Heather whenever she was requested to do so, when Heather called on the morning of Christmas Eve, Megan called Connor at work.

"I want you to know that Heather's asked to see the baby today and I'm driving him over there now," she told him. "I just wanted you to know so you wouldn't accuse me of going behind your back again."

"I know I should be grateful for that much, but is there any way I can persuade you to let me meet you there? Mom, Heather and I need to talk."

"I know that," she said. "But once again she specifically asked me not to tell you where she is. I am going to try to persuade her to spend Christmas with us tomorrow. Don't count on it, though."

"Believe me, if I were in her shoes, I'd turn down that invitation, too," Connor said wryly.

"Why?"

"Too much pressure. It's best if we see each other without an audience."

"I suppose I can understand that. I just thought that perhaps Christmas would be the perfect time for a reconciliation. Besides, she shouldn't be all alone on a holiday."

"I'm not suggesting that you shouldn't try to coax her into coming. I'm just saying I get why she probably won't." He hesitated. "I'd be willing to take the baby and spend the day with her, though. Tell her that, okay? Just the three of us, wherever she wants. It doesn't even have to be where she's staying, so I still won't know where to find her."

Megan heard the vulnerable note in his voice and knew how much it would mean to him to be with his makeshift family on the holiday. "I'll do my best," she said. "I promise."

But when she made the offer to Heather an hour later, Heather turned her down flat.

"I know you mean well, and I want to see Connor, but I can't do it. Not even if it means not seeing my baby on his first Christmas." There was no mistaking the sorrow and disappointment in her eyes when she said it. Then she brightened and pulled a brightly wrapped package from a bag beside her.

"Look, sweet boy," she whispered. "Look what Mommy bought for you for Christmas."

The baby grabbed onto the ribbon and tugged. Heather helped him with the wrapping paper, then grinned when he refused to be diverted from playing with the ribbon.

"I guess what they say is true," she said. "When they're this little, they really don't care about what's inside the box."

Megan laughed. "He will when he finally sees it," she said. She'd seen how much her own children had loved the oversize ball with all the different shaped pieces that could be dropped into the appropriate holes. They'd played with it for hours, brows furrowed until they fit each piece into the right slot, then clamored for her to dump them out again. Of course, they'd been a bit older than little Mick before they'd totally grasped the concept. Until then, they'd just liked throwing the bright plastic shapes on the floor, then crying till she or Mick had picked them up.

Megan eventually glanced at her watch. "Heather, I hate to do this, but I need to get back to help Nell with tonight's dinner, and then we all have to get ready for church."

Heather's expression was so woebegone that Megan almost relented and stayed longer.

"Maybe a few more minutes," she said at last.

Heather shook her head. "No, I don't want you to have to drive home after dark. They're saying we could get snow tonight." Her expression brightened. "Wouldn't it be wonderful to have a white Christmas?" She touched the baby's cheek. "He's never seen snow before. I wish I could be there for that and to see him tomorrow morning when he sees the tree and all the presents."

"Sweetie, you can be there for all of that. I can

convince Connor to declare a truce for the holiday. You won't have to discuss anything that's going on just for tomorrow."

"I wish it could be that easy," Heather said. "I know Connor, though. No matter what promises he makes, he'll insist on pushing the issue and we'll wind up fighting. I don't want my son's first Christmas to be ruined by having his parents creating a scene."

"Trust me, the O'Briens have seen more than their share of scenes through the years," Megan told her.

"But my baby hasn't, and I want it to stay that way. He might be too young to understand what's going on, but he'll sense the tension."

Megan understood her decision. On one level, she even agreed with it, but it reminded her of too many Christmases when she'd avoided her family solely to keep the peace. She'd lived to regret it.

"I hope you won't regret this someday," she told Heather. "Christmas is the perfect time to heal wounds and look for miracles. If you won't come to us, how about going to visit your family?"

Heather shook her head, a look of sorrow washing over her face. "Not an option. They don't approve of any of the decisions I've made since Connor and I moved in together. If I show up without the baby and without a ring on my finger, it'll just be one long day of I-told-you-so. I can't deal with that now."

Megan gave Heather a hug. "If you change your mind, there's always room for one more at our table."

When she released the young woman, there were tears in Heather's eyes. "I wish my mother was half as understanding as you are."

"It's only because I've been where you are," Megan told her. "I left my children for someone else to raise." She tucked a finger under Heather's chin and met her gaze. "And regretted it every day since. Promise me you'll think about that while you're deciding what to do next."

Heather nodded.

"Merry Christmas, sweetie."

Again, Heather blinked back tears. "Merry Christmas," she whispered, then pressed a kiss to her son's forehead. "You, too, little one. Mommy loves you more than anything."

As Megan drove away, she couldn't think of a sadder image than the one she had of Heather in her rearview mirror, shoulders slumped, cheeks damp with tears as she raised her hand in a final wave as the car turned the corner.

Somehow, someway she had to bring this family back together. She just wished she had the first clue about how to pull that off.

14

When Megan arrived back in Chesapeake Shores, she found Connor on the porch watching for her, even though there was a bitter cold breeze off the bay.

"You should be inside," she scolded when he'd crossed the yard to the car. "You'll catch pneumonia in this weather."

"I'm fine," he insisted as he removed little Mick from his car seat and held him as if he'd feared not seeing him again.

Megan studied him with concern. "Connor, are you okay?"

"Fine," he said tersely, then sighed. "I guess I was a little worried."

"About what?"

"That you might get all sentimental because it's Christmas Eve and leave the baby with Heather."

Megan saw the genuine relief in his eyes and was glad she hadn't made that decision, hadn't even considered it, in fact. "Connor, I might empathize with Heather, but I wouldn't have done something like that to you."

"You really mean that, don't you?"

His surprise made her incredibly sad for the second time that afternoon. "You're my son. I love you. I only want what's best for you and your son. And, so you know, Heather never asked me to consider leaving the baby with her. This is where she wants him to be for now."

"But you couldn't persuade her to come back here with you, could you? Not even to spend Christmas Day?"

She shook her head. "She was afraid you two would wind up arguing and it would ruin the holiday."

As they walked inside together, Connor turned and gave her a plaintive look. "You've seen Heather twice now. I'm guessing you've talked about more than the baby. Do you think we're ever going to work this out?"

"I suppose it depends on how much each of you is willing to compromise," she told him. She hesitated, then met his gaze. "We could talk about what you really want, how you see your future. Maybe I could help you see things more clearly."

She could see he was about to refuse, so she quickly added, "Or you could talk and I could just listen. No advice unless it's asked for."

Connor smiled at that. "Do you have any idea how many times you made that promise to me when I was a kid? You'd lure me in with that promise and Gram's cookies, and the next thing you knew, I'd be blabbing away." He met her gaze, but for once there was no animosity in his expression, just a faint hint of nostalgia. "And you never did keep your end of the bargain. You always had an opinion."

"No," she corrected, laughing. "I always had sage advice, which I only offered after you asked for it."

"That is not how I remember it," he insisted, then sighed. "But I have to admit it was always good advice."

"Then maybe we could talk a little now," she said hopefully.

Still, he hesitated. "I have to get the baby down for a nap if he's going to make it through the church service later without fussing."

"That'll give me just enough time to make the hot chocolate and put out a plate of cookies," she told him. She hated begging, but she felt as if they were so close to reconnecting. She didn't want to blow this opportunity. "Please, Connor. I've missed those talks of ours." She felt the tug of a smile on her lips. "I've even missed the arguing. You were always very good at making your case. I should have known then that you'd be an outstanding attorney."

"And you were always just as good at sticking to your guns when I was trying to talk you into letting me do something you didn't approve of."

"I really want us to be able to communicate like that again," she told him.

She waited for what felt like an eternity before he responded.

"Extra marshmallows in the hot chocolate?" he asked.

She beamed at him. "Is there any other way?"

* * *

Mick had seen Megan drive up, then seen Connor rush out to meet her. When he saw his son take the baby upstairs, he walked into the kitchen and found Megan at the stove.

"Everything okay?" he asked.

When she turned around, she had the brightest smile he'd seen in a while on her face.

"Connor and I are going to have a heart-to-heart chat," she said excitedly. "Oh, Mick, this could be the breakthrough I've been hoping for."

As happy as he was about the news and the promise it held, he worried that she was setting herself up for disappointment. "Maybe I should stick around to mediate just in case."

"Just in case of what?" she demanded. "It's a mother and son talking to each other like two adults. We'll be fine."

"It's a mother putting a lot on the line to talk to a son who isn't always reasonable," he corrected. "I just don't want him showing any disrespect to you."

"I can handle whatever he has to say," she insisted. "Besides, it's not going to be about us. Not really. We're going to talk about Heather and their future."

Mick didn't even attempt to hide his surprise. "I hope you can get it through that thick skull of his that he needs to marry that woman."

Megan gave him a wry look. "You haven't even met her. How do you know marriage would be the right decision for either one of them?"

"She's the mother of his child. That's all I need to know."

"Well, I don't intend to tell him what to do. I plan to listen. Now go away before you ruin everything."

"On one condition," Mick said, still reluctant to leave. "You and I sit down later and make some decisions of our own."

She didn't pretend not to understand. "We'll talk," she agreed, pushing him toward the door as they heard Connor approach. "Now go."

Connor gave him a puzzled look as he backed out of the kitchen. "Going somewhere?" he asked Mick.

"Your mother says I am," Mick said, disgruntled.

Connor grinned. "All these years and you still can't handle her," he commented. "I think I'm beginning to see why you love her."

Mick scowled at him. "My relationship with your mother is none of your concern. Just see that you behave in here. She's got her hopes set on the two of you having some kind of breakthrough conversation. Don't let her down."

Connor sobered. "Dad, I can't promise—"

"Do *not* let her down," Mick repeated.

He had a hunch his own future might be depending on it.

How many times had she sat in this very kitchen, biting her tongue and willing her younger son to open up to her? As a boy, Connor had hidden his feelings behind the carefree facade that fooled them all. Now, as she waited for the young man to talk, she could see signs of all those childhood insecurities that lurked just below the confident show he put on.

Because he seemed content to sip his hot chocolate and break off chunks of cookies, she finally broke the ice.

"Heather loves you, you know."

Her words lit up his face for a heartbeat before he quickly covered the reaction with an indifferent shrug. "She has a funny way of showing it."

"Actually she's showing it the same way I did when I left your father. I loved him beyond all reason, despite the way he'd neglected all of us by running off on one business trip after another. In a twisted way, I thought I was giving him his freedom to do the work that he loved without the guilt of coming home to an increasingly unhappy wife."

Connor looked perplexed by the comment. "I don't get it."

"For the longest time, I thought it was easy for him to walk away from us, that he loved his work more than us. I finally realized it wasn't like that at all. He thought he needed to do more and more jobs to succeed *for* us. It dawned on me he thought we expected that from him, when all we really wanted, all *I* really wanted, was for him to be home more. And whenever I tried to tell him any of that, somehow I just added to the pressure he was under."

"Okay, so it's sort of like the O. Henry story," Connor concluded. "You left to take away the pressure on Dad. He worked harder to provide for us. Wouldn't a conversation have fixed everything? He'd have known you didn't care about the material things. You'd have known he loved us more than work."

She grinned at the simplification. "You're right. Solutions always start with honest communication. Unfortunately, I'd spent too many years trying to tell your father what he wanted to hear, or what I thought he wanted to hear. It muddied the waters."

"And you think this somehow applies to me and Heather?"

She nodded. "I know it does. You've said so many times how you feel about marriage that she left so you wouldn't feel pressured by her desire to have a real family with you."

"I do feel strongly about marriages not working," he said. "I see the proof on a daily basis. Am I supposed to ignore that?"

Megan thought carefully before responding. "Connor, you should never ignore what you truly believe. Those beliefs make you who you are. However, sometimes we get so caught up in principles and values and beliefs that we ignore the most important thing of all."

"What's that?"

"How we feel in our heart. If you love this woman, and I believe you do, then you have to find a middle ground that works for both of you." She met his gaze. "Or you have to love her enough to let her go."

Connor regarded her with so much sorrow in his eyes that Megan wanted to hug him fiercely and tell him things would work out, but she didn't know that they would. It was up to him and to Heather.

She did risk covering his hand with hers and giv-

ing his a squeeze. "It will work out the way it's supposed to. I believe that."

"And you believe that about you and Dad, too?"
he asked.

She nodded. "I always have."

"Then marry him, Mom. I won't stand in your
way."

Tears filled her eyes. "Thank you."

"You act as if I really had a choice," he said, though
a smile took the sting out of his words. "I may be
stubborn, but I'm not an idiot. Dad's not going to
rest until he can get you in front of a minister. You
seem to make him happy. I may be skeptical about it
working out, but who am I to be the roadblock? I've
at least learned enough to know that people should
hold on to happiness when they've found it."

There was a new maturity in his voice. His words
might not carry the weight of conviction, but they
meant the world to her just the same. "We can wait
until you're completely reconciled to this," she reminded him.

"I may never be completely reconciled," he admitted. "But I'm not going to stand in your way. You
have my blessing." He grinned at her. "Now go tell
Dad, in case he hasn't managed to hear every word

we've said. I suspect he's outside the door twisting himself into knots trying to eavesdrop."

"If he is, then he should have to wait a little lon- ger before he hears my decision," Megan said. "It's Christmas Eve and Nell is probably champing at the bit to get in here and get dinner on the table before we go to church."

Connor started for the door, then came back to give her an awkward hug that felt more meaningful than any of the impulsive hugs he'd bestowed as a boy. "I'm glad we talked," he told her.

She touched his cheek and tried to blink back tears. "So am I."

In fact, it was the best possible Christmas gift she could have received.

Mick knew something had changed after Megan spent much of the afternoon locked away in the kitchen with Connor. She looked lighter tonight, as if her mind were at ease. At church she sang out with the full-bodied soprano that had always cheered him. There was so much joy in her voice.

He bent down and whispered in her ear. "Things went okay with Connor?"

"Better than okay," she admitted, then silenced

him with a look as the familiar service filled the church with music and the kind of hope that always seemed more powerful at this time of year.

When they walked outside, there was a bitter chill in the air, but the stars were bright in the midnight sky.

"We'll see you first thing in the morning," Abby promised as the family hugged on the church steps and prepared to go their separate ways.

"I can't wait to see what Santa brought me," Davy said, bouncing up and down excitedly. "Do you know, Grandpa Mick? Do you think he got my letter?"

"I know he did," Mick assured him, then winked at Henry. "Yours, too. But you need to get to bed so Santa can sneak in and leave all those presents."

Though Caitlyn and Carrie had claimed their disdain for the whole Santa myth, they still had enough doubt to have them grabbing their mother's hands.

"Mom, let's hurry," Carrie pleaded. "We have to sleep really fast."

Abby laughed. "That's our cue," she said. "Gram, would you like to ride home with us? I think Dad's hoping for some alone time with Mom."

Mick grinned at her. "Way to blow my plans," he grumbled as Megan gave him a curious look.

"Shouldn't we be going straight home, too?" Megan asked. "It's late."

"Not for a couple of free-spirited people like us," he insisted. "I thought we could go for a little drive."

"A drive? At this hour?"

He took her hand in his. "Trust me."

She met his gaze. "Always."

They hugged everyone good-night, then walked toward Mick's car.

"Mick O'Brien, what do you have up your sleeve?" Megan asked as he settled her in the passenger seat.

"Just a little quiet time, so we can make our plans," he said.

Megan fell silent as he drove to a secluded spot on a cliff just beyond The Inn at Eagle Point. "Remember the first time we came up here?" he asked as he parked the car. He reached into the backseat for a bottle of champagne.

"It was the night you told me you were going to build Chesapeake Shores," she said. "I remember thinking you were crazy, that no one sets out to build an entire town from the ground up. I should have known you could do it." Her gaze narrowed. "You don't have some other big announcement, do you?"

"Not an announcement," he said. "I've seen how

you've been lighting up at being surrounded by family this holiday season. I'm wondering if any of that goodwill might spill over to me."

"If I've been in a good mood lately, it's mostly because of you," she told him. "You've given me back my family, Mick. I have a full, rich life again. Even if I never succeed in getting that gallery up and running, I'll be okay."

"You can have it all, if you'd just—"

She smiled and touched a finger to his lips. "I'm turning that one over to God. If it's the right thing, I'll find a way to make it happen."

He took heart from that. "Okay, then, but as good as things are, they could be even better." He poured champagne for the two of them. "Normally I don't condone drinking and driving, but I'm thinking one toast just up the street from our home wouldn't be inappropriate. Here's to us, Meggie, and the future we can build together."

She sipped from her glass. "As excellent as this champagne is, something tells me you didn't bring me up here just so we could share a private toast."

He chuckled. "You know me too well."

"Something you'd do well to remember," she replied.

"Well, as you may recall, one week from tonight we have a wedding scheduled," he said casually, then held her gaze. "Are you planning to show up?"

She regarded him with a startled expression. "Mick, I've been telling you for weeks now that we need to wait. That hasn't changed, at least not entirely."

"What does that mean?"

"I had a really good talk with Connor this afternoon," she began, looking as if she might burst with excitement. "Oh, Mick. It's wonderful! He's given us his blessing."

"Well, hallelujah!" Mick said. "Not that I needed it, but I know you felt it was important. If he's not standing in our way, then what's the problem? Let's get this show on the road!"

Megan laughed. "You are such a guy," she said. "Nothing's planned. That's the problem."

"*Everything's* planned," he corrected. "All I need is the go-ahead from you."

Megan regarded him with a stunned expression. "I don't understand. I thought you knew that one of the biggest problems we have is the way you take over and just ignore the rest of us to get your own way. Now you've obviously gone and done it again.

If and when we get married, Mick, I want a say in the kind of wedding we have."

"Believe me, I've gotten that message loud and clear," he assured her.

"Then why would you move forward without saying a word to me?"

"You've been distracted," he said. "And I have a pretty good notion of what you want."

She looked skeptical. "Oh, really? What kind of flowers do I want in my bouquet?"

"Lilies of the valley just like the ones you planted along the walkway outside. You love that scent so much, it's in the perfume you wear."

She blinked at that. "Okay, that's a lucky guess. What about my dress?"

"Abby spoke to your tailor in New York. She took her a picture you'd admired and the dress is hanging in a closet at her house right now."

"Bridesmaids?"

"Carrie and Caitlyn claimed those spots. Abby has their red velvet dresses, as well."

"What about the cake? I'm very particular about the kind of cake I'd like."

Mick chuckled. "Which you'd apparently made plain to Jess and Gail at the inn weeks and weeks ago. It'll be exactly as you wanted it, right down to the raspberry cream filling."

He could see that she was rapidly running out of objections, but he waited. "Anything more?"

"I never picked out invitations," she said eventually, obviously seizing at straws.

"Because you said we didn't need them if we were only inviting family," Mick said, barely containing a smile. "And to save you the trouble of hunting for more excuses, I've hired the band you liked from last summer's concert series on the green, the reception dinner will have your favorite prime rib as the main course. The only thing I'm not telling you now is where we're going on our honeymoon. That's a surprise."

She studied him with shining eyes. "You've thought of everything, haven't you?"

"I've tried. Don't you get it by now? I will do anything within my power to make you happy. If you want a guarantee, I'll give you one, in writing if you'd prefer it that way."

A full-fledged smile broke across her face. "Then I suppose I've run out of excuses," she told him. She reached up and touched his cheek. "I do love you,

Mick, more than ever. I have no idea why I was being so stubborn."

He laughed at that. "I do. It runs in the family."

Christmas morning dawned with an inch of snow on the ground. It wasn't much, but it added to the excitement as kids ran in and out of the house and Bing Crosby's "White Christmas" played over and over again.

Megan sat next to Mick as wrapping paper and ribbons were tossed in the air amid excited squeals. When Davy opened the package with a baseball mitt, he let out a whoop and ran to his father. "Daddy, see, I told you Santa wouldn't forget. He just left it here instead of at our house."

Kevin grinned at him. "So I see. What about you, Henry? Did Santa leave something special here for you?"

Henry looked up at him with wide eyes. "It's the sports video game I wanted. It has baseball and bowling and everything. Can we play?"

"Of course you can," Connor said, looking as eager as the kids. "I'll set it up in the den. Dad, you coming?"

"On my way," Mick said, then turned and stole

another kiss from Megan. "Just to tide me over till later."

As soon as he'd left the room with all the children and the men, Abby, Bree and Jess surrounded Megan. "Well? Did you say yes last night? I know Dad took champagne up to the cliff and planned to ask you again to marry him. Are we having a wedding New Year's Eve?" Abby demanded.

Megan touched her daughter's cheek, then tucked a wayward curl behind Jess's ear. Before Bree could complain of being neglected, she patted her expanding belly. "Next year we'll have another little one here for Christmas."

A smile spread across Bree's face. "I can hardly wait."

"Mom! You're stalling," Abby protested.

Megan looked at her three precious girls. Right this second she couldn't let herself think of all she'd missed over the years they'd been apart. What mattered was now and all that lay ahead for them as a family.

"Since, according to your father, you all seem to have everything under control," she told them, "then there doesn't seem to be a single reason for me not to go along with the plan." She grinned. "We're having a wedding."

Whoops of happiness greeted the announcement and an instant later, she was enfolded in a group hug that filled her with a joy unlike anything she'd experienced in far too many years. She was within days of having everything she'd ever wanted. Her children were back in her life. Her grandchildren would grow up around her, filling the house with laughter. And the man she'd loved from the moment she'd known the meaning of the word would be by her side forever. It seemed it really was the season of miracles.

Epilogue

The Inn at Eagle Point had been decorated for the holidays with twinkling lights in all of the surrounding trees and shrubs. Inside, the staircase railings were trimmed with fragrant boughs of evergreens and more lights. An eight-foot-tall tree filled the foyer with the scent of pine and the golden glow of white lights, sparkling gold ornaments and flowing gold ribbons. Chunky white candles and slender tapers burned on every tabletop. It was an elegant, fairy-tale setting for a wedding.

Carrie and Caitlyn could barely contain their

excitement as they waited to walk down the aisle. They'd been practicing for days.

Megan stood just outside the door of the room that had been chosen for the ceremony, her heart in her throat.

"Stop fidgeting," Abby instructed. "You'll muss your dress."

Megan ran her hand over the slender, cream-colored satin sheath that had been custom made for her, thanks to Abby. The simple scoop neckline was awash with beads and tiny pearls that sparkled and shimmered in the candlelight.

"What if he changed his mind?" she asked, unable to dismiss her fear that the evening could yet be ruined.

"He'll be here, Mom," Abby said for the tenth time.

"I know he said he'd do it," Megan agreed, her worried gaze searching the hallway.

Then she saw them, Kevin *and* Connor walking toward her, ready to escort her down the aisle.

"You're late," she scolded mildly, then kissed their cheeks. "But I am so glad you're here."

"You try getting someplace on time with a baby," Connor grumbled. "He kept crying and calling for Ga-ma. My son can't say Mama or Da-Da, but he knows what to call you. You've stolen that kid's heart."

Megan regarded him with a misty-eyed look. "And he's healed ours." She searched her son's face. "Hasn't he?"

Connor smiled slowly. It was the carefree expression she'd remembered, but hadn't seen for far too long. "We're okay, Mom."

"Then let's get this show on the road," Kevin grumbled. "This tux is killing me."

"But you look oh-so-handsome," Connor teased. "If I weren't your very straight brother, I'd give you a second look myself."

"Oh, bite me," Kevin retorted.

Megan laughed at the familiar sound of their bickering. It had been like this as far back as she could remember. It was nice that some things would never change.

She urged the twins to begin the walk down the aisle, then linked arms with her sons as the music rose. This was it, the moment she'd feared might never come.

Just as they stepped through the doorway, she winked at Connor. "You're next," she whispered. "I intend to see to it."

That may have been why Connor stumbled on his first step down the aisle. But then his gaze landed on Heather, seated in the back row with his son. Megan saw how his eyes lit up, and knew she'd been right to coax her into coming here tonight.

Then she turned her attention to Mick, waiting impatiently at the front of the room, and everything else faded as she walked toward her future.

* * * * *

**Don't miss the next instalment of Sherryl Woods'
Chesapeake Shores series, the heart-warming
*Driftwood Cottage***

Single mum Heather Donovan's dreams of home and family
are tantalisingly within reach when she settles in Chesapeake
Shores. Unfortunately, this seems to further alienate her son's
father, Connor O'Brien, who is too jaded to believe in
marriage or happy endings.

Then everything changes. Will the possibility of a future without Heather make Connor look at love differently? Heather's
just about given up on her old dreams—of love, of family and
especially of Driftwood Cottage, the home she secretly wishes
was hers. It's going to take a lot of persuasion to make Heather
believe that some dreams are worth fighting for…

Read on for a preview of

DRIFTWOOD COTTAGE

Heather Donovan propped open the front door and stood just inside the brightly lit storefront in Chesapeake Shores so she could inhale the scent of sea air from the bay across Shore Road. Turning slowly, she studied the stacks of colorful fabric bolts that had to be sorted and displayed, the unopened boxes of quilting supplies and the quilt racks that still required assembly. Her pride and joy, the carefully crafted shelving units, had been built to her specifications by her son's grandfather, famed architect Mick O'Brien, for whom her son, little Mick, was named.

Seeing it all coming together was a little overwhelming. Not just opening a business, but all of it—moving to this quaint town, deciding to raise her son on her own, giving up on a future with Connor O'Brien—these were all huge steps. Her mind still reeled when she thought about the recent changes in her life. She might embrace the changes, but that didn't mean she wasn't scared to death.

If anyone had told her a few months ago that she would leave the man she loved more than anything, that she would take their son and move from Baltimore to a small seaside town and embark on a whole new career, Heather would have laughed at the absurdity of the predictions. Even though Connor stubbornly had refused to consider marriage, she'd thought they had a good life, that they were committed to one another. She'd believed that so strongly that she'd ignored her parents'—actually it had been mostly her mother's—warnings about the mistake she was making by having a child with Connor without a ring on her finger.

But, in fact, they—she, Connor and their son—might have gone on exactly like that for years if she hadn't seen how Connor's career as a divorce lawyer was chipping away at their relationship, how his anger at his parents was corrupting their day-to-day lives. She didn't like the embittered man she'd seen him becoming, and he seemed to have no desire to change.

It wasn't as if she'd made her decision to break up lightly. She'd gone away for several weeks, leaving their son with Connor's family while she'd pondered what was best for her future and for her child's. She hadn't been happy about the conclusion she'd reached, that she needed to start a new life on her own, but she'd made peace with it. And, in time, she knew she'd find the fulfillment that had eluded her with Connor.

Not that she could envision a day when she'd stop loving him, she thought even now, months after making the decision. She sighed at how difficult it sometimes was to reconcile emotions with common sense and facing reality, especially with a precious little boy as a constant reminder of what she'd given up.

A bell over the shop's front door tinkled merrily, interrupting her thoughts. Megan O'Brien stepped inside, carrying her grandson who beamed at the sight of Heather.

"Mama!" he cried, holding out his chubby little arms. Just over a year old now, he was the joy of Heather's life.

"He was missing you," Megan explained, then gave her a commiserating look. "And I thought you might be needing a glimpse of him about now. I know you're still not over all those weeks the two of you spent apart."

"Thank you," Heather said, reaching for her son.

"Feeling overwhelmed?" Megan asked with the kind of insight that Heather had come to treasure.

So many times in the past few months she'd regretted that Megan wouldn't be her mother-in-law. In many ways Heather felt closer to Connor's mother than she did to her own mother back in Ohio. A wonderful salt-of-the-earth woman who went to church on Sundays, volunteered at a homeless shelter and in a children's hospital, Bridget Donovan had an endless store of compassion for everyone except her own daughter. She flatly refused to accept that any daughter of hers would willingly choose not to marry the father of her child.

Heather sighed. As if marriage to Connor had ever been an option, no matter how desperately she might have hoped for it.

Heather bounced baby Mick in her arms as she nodded in response to Megan's question. "You're right about feeling overwhelmed," she said, gesturing around the store. "I have no idea where to start. What if opening a shop, especially here, is a huge mistake? I don't know anything about running a business. And being here, in this town, surrounded by O'Briens, what was I thinking? Why on earth did I let you talk me into this?"

"Because you knew it was a brilliant idea," Megan said at once, obviously still pleased with herself for coming up with this solution for Heather's future.

"Still, doubts are understandable," she consoled Heather. "You've made a lot of changes recently. All good ones, I think. As for starting your own business, this is a natural fit for you. The minute I saw those handmade quilts of yours, I knew it. You do absolutely beautiful work. Everyone in town is going to want to own one of your quilts or have you teach them how to make their own."

Megan fingered a small folk art quilt of a bay scene as she spoke. "This one, for instance, is a treasure. How can you bear to part with it? And at this price? It needs to cost twice as much."

"The price is fine. I was just experimenting," Heather said modestly, still astonished that anyone thought her hobby could turn into a thriving business. She had always enjoyed quilting, and it had filled the quiet evenings while Connor studied. She'd never envisioned it as anything more than a hobby.

In fact, her college degree had been in literature. She'd never quite figured out what to do with that besides teach. After two years in an out-of-control Baltimore high school classroom, she'd gratefully quit when she'd become pregnant with Connor's baby.

She gestured to the quilt Megan was admiring. "If you aren't just saying that to calm me down, if you really like it, I'll make one for you."

Megan's eyes brightened. "I'd love it, but I will pay you

for it, and I swear I'm going to talk you into doubling the price."

"Absolutely not."

"Well, that's what I'm paying," Megan countered just as stubbornly. "You've a business to run, after all."

Heather sighed. "Starting a business is just one of my concerns these days," she admitted. "What about moving out on Connor? Was that the right decision, Megan?" She couldn't seem to keep a wistful note out of her voice.

"Even that," Megan assured her. "My son is stubborn, and you've given him exactly the wake-up call he needed." She patted Heather's hand. "He loves you. Just tuck that knowledge away. He'll come around if you're patient."

"For how long?" Heather asked. "We met our freshman year in college, dated for four years, moved in together when he was in law school. When I found out I was pregnant, I was so sure we'd get married, especially when he encouraged me to quit my job to be a full-time mom. I was certain we were finally going to be a real family, the kind I'd always wanted. He even said that's what he wanted, too, just without a marriage license."

She waved off her regrets. "I should have known better than to expect him to change his mind. Connor always told me he had no intention of ever marrying, that he didn't believe in marriage. It's not as if I didn't understand the rules from the very beginning."

"People don't make rules about things like that," Megan said dismissively. "They just let the past control the future. In Connor's case, his attitude is all because of what happened between his father and me. Now that Mick and I have remarried and started over, I'm convinced

Connor will see that love can endure all kinds of trials, including divorce."

Heather smiled at her optimism. "Have you met Connor? He's stubborn as a mule. Once he gets an idea into his head, he won't let go of it. And look how long it's been since I moved out. It was last Thanksgiving when I left to think things over, January when I officially left him. It'll be Easter soon, and he still hasn't shown any signs of changing his mind. He may not be entirely happy that I'm gone, but he's not doing anything at all to change the situation."

Megan grinned. "I'm married to a man just like that, his father. Believe me, there are ways of getting through to their hard heads." She glanced pointedly at the boy in Heather's arms. "And you've your ace in the hole right there. Connor adores his son."

Heather shook her head. "A couple can't build a future around a child. It's not fair. My parents did that. They stayed in a miserable marriage because of me. They thought it would be best, but it wasn't. The tension was unbearable. I won't have that for my son."

"I'm not suggesting that you be together for your child, only that he'll keep you in Connor's orbit while he gets his feet back under him and realizes how much he loves you both. Having you with him was entirely too comfortable. He had it all his own way. The stance you've taken is the smart one. Eventually he'll realize what he needs to do to have the two of you back again."

"I hope you're right," Heather admitted, though she wasn't counting on it. In fact, if things didn't work out with Connor, it could make her decision to move to Chesapeake Shores where she'd be surrounded by his family the worst one she'd made in years. The O'Briens might provide an enviable support system, but she'd be reminded of what could have been every minute of every day.

"Of course I'm right," Megan said confidently. "Now tell me what I can do to help you get organized in here. Do you have a system?"

Even to her own ears, Heather's laugh had an edge of hysteria about it. "If only," she said, glancing around at the chaos. She regarded Megan hopefully. "Are you sure you have some time to spare?"

"Of course I do. At Mick's insistence, I've hired a very competent assistant at the gallery, and things are under control. In the meantime, I'll let her know I'll be right next door if she needs me," she said, flipping open her cell phone. When she'd made the call, she told Heather, "Now, just put me to work."

Heather didn't hesitate. "If you could start opening those boxes, I could begin sorting the fabric for the displays," she suggested, settling Mick into the playpen she'd already set up in a corner. He uttered an immediate howl of protest, then spotted one of his favorite toys and was quickly absorbed with that.

Heather and Megan worked in companionable silence for a while before Megan inquired, "Have you told Connor about the shop yet? He didn't mention it last time we spoke and I certainly didn't want to be the one to fill him in."

Heather stiffened. "It hasn't come up. Truthfully, we barely exchange a dozen words when I drop Mick off to spend the day with him. I haven't even told him I've moved here. He reaches me on my cell phone when he needs to, so it's not as if it really matters where I've settled. I suppose if I'd run off to California, he might have a legitimate complaint, but I'm barely an hour away. Nothing's changed in terms of his schedule to see little Mick."

Megan looked distressed by her response. "Oh, Heather, you need to tell him," she said. "And you need to do it before he comes home for a visit and discovers it for himself or before someone else in the family blabs. He'll be furious that you've kept it from him."

Heather shrugged. "It'll just be one more thing to add to the list. He's already angry that I refused to move back in. To be honest, he wasn't all that happy when I insisted on keeping little Mick with me after I'd left him here with you while I was trying to sort through things and get my head on straight. He apparently thought the arrangement was going to be permanent."

"There's no question that he liked having the baby here with him and the rest of the family," Megan acknowledged. "We all did. But I think everyone except Connor understood it was only temporary."

Heather regarded her with sorrow. "Sometimes I think I'm destined to keep making things worse between Connor and me. If we talk at all, we're at odds over everything."

Megan smiled at that. "It's only awkward right now because you won't give him what he wants—an unconditional commitment that doesn't include marriage. He has to learn that he can't always have things on his own terms."

"But aren't I doing the same thing, expecting to have things on *my* terms?" Heather asked.

Megan regarded her thoughtfully. "I suppose that's

true. Maybe it's just because I think you're the one who's right that I'm not blaming any of this standoff on you. I think two people who love each other and have a child together ought to at least try marriage, that they ought to be fighting to make it work."

She sighed. "Goodness knows, I spent years trying to make things work with Mick before I took the drastic step of leaving. Even in hindsight, I don't think I had a choice by then, though I know I should have handled things differently and much better where all of our children were concerned. I still regret that, and I'd never have forgiven myself if I'd simply run at the first sign of trouble, rather than leaving as a last resort."

Heather grinned at her. "But here you are, together again. Happy endings still happen. Why can't Connor see that, especially when it's right in front of his face?"

"I fear it's because he doesn't have a romantic bone in his body," Megan replied sorrowfully. "He's become cynical when it comes to love. Mick and I did that to him, and that job of his—dealing with bitter divorces every single day—has reaffirmed his jaded views."

"Then what makes you think he'll ever come around?" Heather asked.

Because I *am* a romantic," Megan said, smiling.

Can a single moment change your entire life?

International lawyer Sophie Bellamy has dedicated her life to helping people in war-torn countries. But when she survives a hostage situation, she remembers what matters most—the children she loves back home. Haunted by regrets, she returns to the idyllic Catskills village of Avalon on the shores of Willow Lake, determined to repair the bonds with her family.

www.mirabooks.co.uk

A touch of Christmas magic!

Beth Morehouse was expecting presents under the tree, not a basket of abandoned puppies on the doorstep of 1225 Christmas Tree Lane!

To top off her Christmas worries, the girls have invited their dad, Beth's ex-husband, Kent, for the holidays. Clearly they have visions of a mum-and-dad reunion under the mistletoe. But Kent's new girlfriend might have other ideas...

Brimming with mistletoe and festive miracles, there's nothing like Christmas in Cedar Cove!

Make time for friends.
Make time for Debbie Macomber.

Home, heart and family. Sherryl Woods knows what truly matters

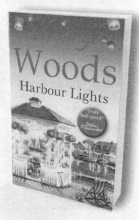

Struggling in his role as a newly single father, former army medic Kevin O'Brien moves home to Chesapeake Shores in search of a haven for himself and his son.

Main Street bookseller Shanna immediately recognises Kevin as a wounded soul—and, with his little son in arms, Kevin is almost impossible to resist.

Confronted with a threat to their hard-won serenity when someone from Shanna's past appears, Kevin and Shanna face their toughest challenge— learning to trust again.

HARLEQUIN® MIRA®
www.mirabooks.co.uk

M274_HL

**Healing families, healing hearts.
In Chesapeake second chances
happen in the most
unexpected ways.**

Bree had dreamt of seeing her name in bright
lights on Broadway, but her dreams are fading.
Going home is the perfect safe haven; she needs
time to wrap herself in her family's love
and forget everything.

But not all is peaceful and serene. Her ex–boyfriend
is demanding answers. Bree had given Jake Collins
plenty of reasons to want her out of his life,
but now she's right back in it. Is she
home for good?

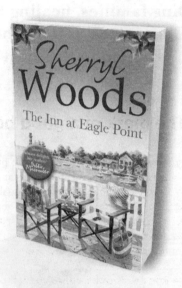

It's been years since Abby O'Brien Winters set foot
in Chesapeake Shores. But one panicked phone
call from her youngest sister brings her racing back
home to protect Jess's dream of renovating the
Inn at Eagle Point.

But saving the inn means dealing not only
with her own fractured family, but also with
Trace Riley, the man Abby left ten years ago.
Trace can be a roadblock to her plans…or
proof that second chances happen in the
most unexpected of ways.

M229_TIAEP